TITANOBOA

SHIGERU BRODY

The enormous fish glided silently through the sea. Skimming the surface, it didn't perceive the vibrations of prey nearby. The ocean species scattered when such a large predator neared. The fish tilted its right pectoral fin, almost like a fighter plane, and slowly arched another way. It hadn't eaten for three days, and the hunger inside of it, the hunger that came with pregnancy, was ravenous. This litter was particularly large. Her brain was too small to form the correct thoughts, but somehow, instinctively, she knew that many pups depended on her eating soon.

Her half-moon tail slowly swept from side to side as she attempted to pick up any indication of prey in the water. Gelatinous sacks on her snout, ampullae of Lorenzini, detected the electromagnetic signals all living prey gave off. They could even sense a heartbeat from nearly half a mile away.

Suddenly, the shark stopped, its tail frozen midsweep. It detected a slight movement of muscles that gave off an electrical impulse. Farther down in the sea, it was rising, unaware of the massive fish waiting for it near the surface. The fish decided to sweep around and come up from under the prey. Like a heat-seeking missile, it could launch vertically through the ocean and collide against its prey with such force that their hearts could stop.

The fish swept around but detected something odd. The prey wasn't continuing on its journey up. It had moved directly under the shark.

The fish had never sensed fear. It could comprehend danger, but the only danger in its adult life was around larger sharks. The sea was a safe place for it, and it didn't understand the prey's movements. The fish just swam farther out, still attempting to get underneath the prey.

But, as it had last time, the prey followed it.

The fish exhibited only two reactions in a situation that confused it: fight or flee. And, forced by hunger and the growing pups inside, it decided to fight. It swung down directly at the prey, whose movements it now sensed. The movements had increased; it rose faster. The fish opened its mouth as if in anticipation. They were on a direct collision course.

And then, a jolt of something akin to fear, but not quite, traveled through the great fish. Some deep, prehistoric shock its primitive brain had buried inside of it. A warning that it needed to flee.

The prey was not prey at all. And as the shark began to recognize the enormousness of whatever was rising beneath it, it now understood that it was in the realm of a greater predator. In its hunger, it had made a mistake.

The shark quickly banked left and pounded its tail in a flurry of movement. It sped like a torpedo through the water, its sheer mass creating its own current. The fish could swim at over twenty-five miles per hour, one of the fastest fish in the sea. But the faster predator below it was closing in.

The shark, now panicked, swam closer to the surface, so close that its dorsal fin cut through the water and skimmed the top. It saw clear blue ocean ahead of it. But it had nowhere to go from a quicker predator.

Its tail beat furiously, the tip of the crescent, the

caudal fin, rising from the water. But exhaustion for an animal this size fell quickly. The muscles in its tail weakened, its heart beating so fast it could've burst. It couldn't keep this up for long.

And whatever was underneath it was close.

The shark gave one last push. It veered sharply to the left in a way only a fish in water could. Made almost entirely of cartilage, it could bend in half. In an instant, it was going the same speed in a different direction.

But it didn't matter.

The predator was faster.

Something the shark had never felt tingled within it. It didn't have the brain capacity to identify it, but it was something new. Something unwanted. Fear. For the first time in the great fish's life, it was afraid.

The predator burst underneath it so fast, the shark didn't have time to move. A force against it like a massive wave knocked it clear out of the water into the warm air. Sun blinded it for only an instant, then blackness as something wrapped around it and sucked it back into the ocean.

It wrapped around the entire length of the fish's body, from its caudal fin to its snout. The slithery, slick surface of something touching every part of its body all at once. The shark struggled, trying to whip free. But it felt pain so intensely it could hardly move. Fangs sank into its snout, and whatever had wrapped around its body slowly squeezed. It crushed the great fish, its teeth cracking against each other, its liver exploding with such force it tore open its belly, releasing a cloud of blood and gore.

The shark's last sensation before it died was that of being eaten alive.

1

Professor Craig Millard took the podium and adjusted his Mac before clearing his throat. They had told him to start with a joke, but as he looked out over the sea of faces, all he wanted to do was get through this as quickly as possible.

The symposium was supposed to cater just to herpetologist undergraduates and graduate students, but they weren't the only people in the crowd. Most herpetologists knew about the groupies, people that loved reptiles. He was one of them, but he never kept a dangerous one in his home as most of the groupies did. Reptiles were unpredictable and possessed no emotion. The fact that someone raised it meant nothing.

"Um..." He cleared his throat again. A joke didn't sound that bad. Only one came to mind. "A woman found a snake with a broken back in the road, a rattler. She picked it up and took it into her home. She fed it, cleaned it, took care of it, and eventually the snake got better. When he was fully healed and ready for release back into the wild, the woman lifted him to place him outside, and the snake bit her in the arm. As the woman lay dying on her floor, she asked the snake, 'Why would you do that? I loved you. I took care of you. How could you kill me?' To which the snake replied, 'Listen, chick, you knew I was a snake.'"

A few chuckles emanated from the crowd. Just enough to relax him. He pushed a button on the Mac, and the projection screen behind him displayed a massive serpent in comparison to an elephant, which it dwarfed.

"This is *titanoboa cerrejonensis*. The largest species of snake ever found. It's a recent discovery, but we assume there must've been other snakes in its genus, though we haven't discovered them as yet. After the K-T event, so called because it came right at the end of the Cretaceous and the beginning of the Tertiary in the earth's history... Um, and for those of you that don't know, we use *K* to denote the Cretaceous so it doesn't get confused with the Cambrian and other epochs—that event ended the reign of the dinosaurs about sixty million years ago, and we don't know what species survived and thrived on land. For about ten million years after the K-T event, we simply don't know what lived on this planet. Until we found titanoboa.

"All we've found is a few pieces of vertebrae, but we estimate its size as no more than a hundred feet, although we have no real idea how large they must've grown. A snake never stops growing, not for its entire life. As long as it has food—and adequate heat, since it's cold-blooded—it will grow until its death. Say, by aggressive motorcycle gangs of mongooses."

Another chuckle, this one more subdued. Millard pushed his glasses up farther on his nose as he flipped to another image. This one portrayed a titanoboa eating a prehistoric crocodile.

"The fact is, the older a snake, the larger the snake. Several Amazonian explorers searching for various lost cities, including famed explorer Percy Fawcett, gave us accounts of massive constrictor snakes, the boa and anaconda variety. Some stated there were snakes as large as sixty feet. So it's not out of bounds to estimate that titanoboa, which was likely the top predator of its epoch, could easily have reached two hundred feet or even more. And it'd have to be, based on our projections, about the width of a car to be that long. We can't even guess as to the force an animal like this could generate. Even a small boa could crush every bone in our body. An animal like titanoboa would simply be awe inspiring, or nightmare inspiring, depending on your perspective.

"As far as behavior, we have to, as most of paleontology does, surmise certain things about its behavior based on the conduct of its modern relatives, the boas and anacondas, pythons, et cetera. It must've crushed its prey first, waiting for it to stop movement, and then simply swallowed it whole. One interesting phenomenon that's been seen in the boa family is this urge to regurgitate prey when new prey presents itself. Boas and pythons tend not to do it, but we've seen it in anacondas frequently. We don't know why they do it. Perhaps their brains are too small to understand that they don't need to eat again, or perhaps they, for lack of a better term, enjoy killing. Certainly a possibility in the animal kingdom, as squids have displayed this trait, not to mention our own species of course."

Millard took a drink of water. They'd given him seven minutes, as all the speakers had, and he'd already taken up one and a half. He'd have to cut some of the talk. He decided to focus on ecology, predatory behavior, morphology, and the reason for extinction. The extinction interested him the most.

A top predator like that had no reason to go extinct other than a change in climate. He'd seen in some species of snake the migration from one end of a country to the other as they pursued warmer temperatures. He believed it possible that, as the earth cooled, titanoboa simply followed the warmer temperatures. But it could thrive without migration in places with high mean temperatures. It simply had no reason to be extinct, but that wasn't unusual. 99.9 percent of all species that ever existed had gone extinct, and only a fraction was due to human action. Extinction was the normal process of life, and each species had roughly, based on current estimates, about 4 million years of life before extinction occurred for one reason or other. Considering modern humans had only existed about 200,000 years, he was confident they had a long way to go, as long as they didn't destroy themselves. Which was an ability no other species in history ever had.

The more interesting question was what titanoboa would be like if it had survived. By necessity, it would be more intelligent. At least more intelligent than other snakes. It couldn't avoid detection this long without that. It would need to be a scavenger as well as a hunter and not be selective in its prey. It would have to eat anything that gave it sustenance. And it would probably have gotten larger. Large enough to prey on anything it happened across.

Millard finished his lecture with thirty seconds to spare and thanked the audience as they clapped. He stepped off the stage to allow the next speaker up. He had wanted to stay and hear him, a colleague of his that specialized in amphibian reproduction. He was going to speak about a new method of insemination in frogs that sounded mildly interesting. But Millard felt too wired, as he always did after speaking to a crowd. Something he had gone into biology specifically to avoid.

As he walked around the stage, he decided to sneak out. A question and answer session was slated after all the talks, but he'd just as soon grab some lunch and head back to the airport.

Near the door, a man leaned against the wall with his arms folded. The man wore a suit, an expensive one from the looks of it. He smiled widely. "Dr. Millard. How are ya, brother?"

"Um, fine."

"Doctor," he said, putting his arm around Millard's shoulders as they walked out together, "have I got some news that is gonna make you sweat as much as a whore on nickel night."

2

Mark Whittaker woke with a start. His shirt clung to him, and droplets of sweat rolled down his neck.

He saw the door of his home opened onto the sandy beach of Kalou Island. He tasted the ocean breeze that blew in, salty with a not entirely unpleasant scent of rotting seaweed hanging in it. He peeled off his shirt and hit the shower.

Kalou Island was one of the largest islands in the Republic of Fiji. The year round warmth was to die for. Other than monsoon season, which only lasted a short time. Even in the colder months, the temperatures only dropped to the mid-70s.

After his shower, he dressed and ate a meal of Captain Crunch with almond milk. Fiji was extraordinarily diverse, but they primarily ate Indian cuisine. The spice always hurt Mark's stomach, so he preferred his comfort food. Mostly things he ate as a child.

He finished his bowl of cereal and stepped out into the sunlight. A few families were already out on the beach, and he watched them a moment before putting on his sunglasses and heading to his car. The car was nothing fancy. Few of the year-round natives owned anything fancy and cared almost nothing for luxury items. When

Mark first moved there, it shocked him to learn that if no one cared about what one drove, one tended to look for practicality rather than flash. He realized just how much other people's opinions influenced his decisions back in the States.

Mark lived in Kalou's one major city, Vusa. The population in the off-season hovered around two thousand and swelled to double that with the tourists during the summer months. The city's intersecting streets provided clear addresses so everyone could find whatever they were looking for quickly. The city was much cleaner than any city Mark had ever been to, partly because the people valued the beauty of their island. And partly because the punishment for littering was a day in jail.

As Mark arrived downtown, buildings switched from a light island blue to reds and yellows as he went farther into the city. A purposeful decision by the city's selectmen, the equivalent of a city council, to make sure tourists always felt uplifted and happy while there.

Mark's three-story office building was painted a light blue with depictions of crabs and seashells on the side. The office space rented at one hundred Fijian dollars per month, the equivalent of about fifty U.S. dollars, and came fully furnished with a part-time secretary shared by everyone on his floor.

Island design decorated the interior, with a massive poster of a champion surfer riding a wave on the wall when he walked through the front doors. The carpet was gray and clean. The first floor housed a call center staffed entirely by native islanders. Though Kalou's official language was Fijian, everybody spoke English, one of three official languages of the country as a whole. The native islanders began learning English when they were five, and by the time they graduated middle school, they were as fluent as any American or Brit. Probably more so, from what Mark had seen the last few times he watched American or British television.

He took the stairs up to the second floor's executive suites and walked through the double glass doors of suite 200. An attractive young woman named Zahina sat behind the desk, flipping through something on her computer.

"Any messages?" Mark said.

They played that game occasionally. Mark was the island's only private investigator. A private investigator on an island where things didn't really happen was not exactly an in-demand job. But Kalou boasted exactly three policemen: a chief, a deputy chief, and a uniformed patrol officer. The three of them, though incredibly warm, friendly men, were about the laziest police officers Mark had ever known. Unless a crime committed on the island affected a tourist, the police couldn't really be bothered. Unless of course someone paid a bribe.

The bribes were usually quite high, typically more than Mark's fees, and so a dozen times a year, sometimes less, sometimes more, someone hired Mark for something they needed done. Like investigating who had vandalized their property or stolen their television. He also retained a contract with the chief and was occasionally called out to scenes of car accidents or the more serious crimes and paid by the hour for his services. As former LAPD, he was the only one on the island that had actually gone through a police academy.

Even with all that, he received usually less than four new client calls a month.

"Yes," Zahina said, "the president called. They want

to give you your medal for heroism in the face of danger."

"Excellent, I'll take it in my office. Actually, no... make him wait."

"Your wish is my command."

As he opened his private office's door, he noticed something on Zahina's desk. A clear bowl with a spider inside. The spider was large, probably about the size of the palm of his hand, and sat perfectly still.

"Ew, what'dya have that for?" he asked.

"Just a reminder."

"Of what?"

"Just nature. Our place in it. My dad always kept spiders around and told us stories about how they used to be worshipped. You know, nature's greater than us, and all. He said it kept people humble."

"Nature's greater than us? I don't see any spider cities."

"Not like that, silly. But, you know, we might not be the dominant animals forever."

"Yeah," he said. "Let me know when dolphins make rocket ships, will ya?"

She grinned. "Oh, hey, you did actually have a call. It was a potential client."

"Yeah? Who?"

"Some lady. She's coming in at two to meet with you. It was weird; she wouldn't give me her name. She said she would only talk to you."

Mark stepped into his office, decorated exactly as it had been the day he moved in. A couple plants, a poster of a fire dance or something on the beach, and a desk and chair. He'd chosen this office because right behind his desk, a massive window looked down onto Kamal Street, the main street running through the island. From here, he had a view of all the major shops, the tourists, the bars and restaurants, and just about everything else. Farther out, past downtown and on the outskirts of the city, he could see the green outline of the jungles.

He sat at his desk and turned on his computer. The old PC took nearly five minutes to boot up. Leaning back in the chair, he put his feet up on the desk and stared out the window. Hard to believe that just four years ago he was in a patrol car cruising Watts, chasing down gang-bangers and dope dealers. He charged them with something, got them into a cell, and the next day they were out. The jails were so crowded, if the police didn't deem someone an immediate threat, they had to cut them loose.

Once the computer was running, he opened his email. Exactly one. A message from Amazon recommending different types of firearm holsters based on his past purchases. He perused a few of them, decided his old holster was fine, and picked up a file in a basket on his desk.

One of his open cases was a woman, a summer native only on the island from April until August, who thought her husband was cheating on her with a cocktail waitress at one of the bars. Mark had followed him around for a week and didn't see him do anything but lie on the beach, play tennis, and go to the gym. He thought the woman was nuts until he realized the husband was going to the gym at odd hours. Mark followed him into the gym.

The husband strolled right through the gym and the side door. Mark trailed him there, too. The man rounded a corner, walked straight to a little hotel on the beach, and kissed a beautiful woman in front of the building before going inside.

Mark hadn't told the wife yet, and he wasn't particularly looking forward to that conversation. Those wealthy enough to summer in the islands were a different breed he wasn't quite used to. He saw some of them in Hollywood and the more upscale areas in L.A., but for the most part, he didn't understand how differently the super-rich lived from those that weren't. The fact was, the woman was probably cheating on him as well and looking for extra ammunition in the looming divorce.

Mark flipped through the file, organized his photos, and drafted his official report. He read it twice then printed it out and placed it in the file. He looked to the clock on his desktop. An hour had passed, and it was eleven now.

Precisely sixteen places to eat were in the city, and he was on a sixteen-day rotation through them all. Today was a place near the beach that specialized in seafood. That morning's catch was their menu, written on a chalkboard in blue and green chalk. Mark strolled there, enjoying the heat and the summer breeze, and sat on the veranda.

Tourists were the lifeblood of this island and given special treatment at every turn. But they weren't a bad crowd, not like some he had seen. For the most part, they shopped, they ate, they went to dinner parties and the one nightclub in the city to dance, and that was it. The beaches were like background scenery or a painting. Something for them to look at but not really enjoy. Few tourists, with the exception of those with children, even went down to the beach except to lie on a chair and get sun. They mostly left the water to the locals.

Mark ordered a beer and scallops. The fat, round scallops, the edges wrinkled, arrived with a spicy curry sauce. The scallops still tasted of ocean salt, fried up a little with butter and lemon then served.

He ate all of them then licked his fingers, a habit his wife used to tell him he had to break. At restaurants, she scolded him for doing it and made him feel like a child. He wondered if she did that to her current husband, too.

He checked the clock on his phone then ordered a batch of scallops and a chocolate milk to go. He left a generous tip, which over here wasn't much more than a couple of dollars, and left the restaurant.

The one school in the city, about two blocks outside of downtown, catered to children from kindergarten through middle school. By the time they reached high school, either they had picked out their professions and stopped their education, or they moved to a bigger island to complete it. The school wasn't much more than a large house connected to two other large houses, beautifully sculpted, with trimmed bushes, darkly tiled roofs, and even a corridor with no roof so the children could enjoy the direct sunlight during the day.

Mark sauntered inside the school. The kids were just getting ready for lunch. He went to the cafeteria, and the familiar face he saw every day was there.

"How are you, friend?" Mariah said.

"Good." He handed her the bag with the scallops and milk. "How's everything here?"

"Living the dream." She grinned, not taking her eyes off the food she was preparing. "Hey, you going to that beach party tonight?"

"Which one is that?"

"The one the selectmen are putting on. Some big shot is here from an oil company and they're throwing him a party. Open bars and all the oysters you can eat."

"Wasn't planning on it, but maybe I'll stop by."

She stopped what she was doing and looked at him. "You need to get out of your house sometimes, Mark. It's good to be around other people."

"I'm around other people all the time. I'm here with you, I have a meeting with a client at two, then I'll joke around with my secretary for a while, and then I'll go home. That's plenty."

She shook her head and went back to work. "Suit yourself. But we got some cute girls on this island that have asked about you."

"Tell them I'm spoken for. Whenever you put in for that divorce, I'm ready."

She blushed lightly and chuckled. Though he was kidding—she was twice his age, for one thing—she never let a compliment go unnoticed.

"Have a good one, Mariah."

He ambled around the school and caught a glimpse of the courtyard where the children ate lunch. Kalou didn't have any subsidized lunch programs. The children ate what they brought with them or bought lunches from Mariah.

One day, as Mark was walking by the school, a young boy sat by himself in the corner of the courtyard. Mariah was also a tour guide and had shown him around the island when he'd first arrived, and he asked her about the boy. Nothing unusual about a boy sitting by himself. Mark had been the same way as a child, but the boy was so sullen, so melancholy, that he felt compelled to ask.

Mariah told him the boy's father had run off, leaving him and his mother to fend for themselves. The mother did odd jobs here and there to feed them, but jobs on the island were scarce. The boy, Mariah informed him, ate only one meal a day at home. He had to skip lunch.

So every day, Mark bought two lunches. One for himself and one dropped off at the school for the boy. Mark made Mariah swear she would never tell him where the lunches came from. He didn't want the boy to feel like a charity case. But before noon, without fail for the past two years, he had brought lunch for him.

The boy's face lit up as Mariah waddled over and gave him the lunch. She had been telling him it was just part of the school's program to provide it. The boy immediately opened the chocolate milk and took a long swig before digging into the scallops.

Mark grinned and walked back to his office. He would wait there for the mysterious client to show up.

3

Mark read the *LA Times* in his office. He had grown up there, and he liked to stay abreast of the goings on in the city. Apparently, the city council had voted in favor of English-only schools within the city and then, due to mass protests, had changed their vote and voted against it. Because of backlash from the opposing side, they might reverse their decision again. He had no idea how the hell idiots were always the ones in power.

Two o'clock rolled around, and he waited twenty minutes, browsing a few other websites before he decided this potential client wasn't showing up. But as he turned his computer off and prepared to leave for the day, his secretary buzzed him. "She's here."

"Okay, send her back."

Mark sat down at the desk again. He was suddenly self-conscious about his appearance. He would probably describe it as casual island attire. Definitely no suits or ties involved. Anywhere else, they would probably think he was a bum and wouldn't hire him for a nickel. But in this place, with these people, it was completely expected. He hoped she'd been on the island long enough to realize that.

Kalou's mode of life was much slower. Everyone was expected to take his or her time. No one could take blame for coming into work late or missing particularly nice days when the beach called. Employers and customers predominantly understood things like that. Mark wasn't upset she was late and in fact chastised himself for being so uptight about it.

His door opened, and his secretary led in a young woman. She was perhaps thirty, maybe thirty-two, and wearing a red skirt with nylons and heels. A black top finished off her outfit. Something for an office, not an island, and he guessed she hadn't been here long. Or perhaps she thought this was how one dressed when meeting with a private investigator.

Mark rose and held out his hand. "Mark Whittaker."

"Riki Gilmore, nice to meet you."

They shook hands then sat down across from each other. She crossed her legs and looked him in the eyes. Few people that came into his office did that. Their eyes usually darted around and they fidgeted.

"I was referred to you by Police Chief Koroi. He said you might be able to help me."

"What exactly is it you need help with?"

She pulled up a photo on her phone and handed it to him. On the screen was a young man, perhaps no more than twenty. "My brother. He disappeared here two weeks ago."

"Here as in Vusa?"

"Yes. Well, just outside the city. He was on the beach, Chaundry Beach, and he called me. We spoke for a while, and he hung up. No one's heard from him since. He didn't check back into the hotel, he never called his girlfriend, nothing. He just vanished."

"Hm." Mark handed the phone back to her. "You sure he didn't just lose his phone?"

"No. His girlfriend is pregnant. He'd been calling her several times a day. If he'd lost his phone, he could just call from the hotel until he got a new one. But the hotel said the last time they saw him was that day. Two weeks ago, the day I talked to him. As far as I know, I was the last person to talk to him. His name's Billy Gilmore."

"Where's he from?"

"San Diego. That's where we live. He hasn't called into his job, either. They had to replace him."

Mark leaned back in his seat and glanced out the window at a passing car, an old Buick or Chrysler with rust on the side. "Sorry for asking these questions, but I have to be thorough. Is it possible your brother ran off with another woman?"

"Not a chance. He loves her. Something's happened. I just know it. I flew out here a week ago and went to the police. They don't care. They said they would file a report and look into it, but I don't even know if they've done that."

He shook his head. "Without any evidence of what happened, they won't look too deeply. Have you tried the consulate?"

"They're even worse. They made an entry on their computer and said they would call me if he turned up."

Mark considered his options. Had he been desperate for cash, he would've jumped at the case. But he wasn't wanting for money. His pension from the police force and the few thousand dollars a year he made here were more than enough to meet, and exceed, all his needs. So the only real question was whether he wanted to take the case.

When he finally made detective his last year on the LAPD, he worked for six months in the Missing Persons division. Most MPs were actually just runaways. Or people that had up and left their families without a word to their spouses or children. Murders, kidnappings, and accidental deaths weren't as common. And that was in Los Angeles. He couldn't even imagine the odds against a murder on a small island where everybody was in everybody else's business.

The problem was that, if he actually found Billy and discovered he had run off to Las Vegas or Mexico or somewhere and shacked up with a cocktail waitress, the family would be bitter and angry. And Mark might be the target of that bitterness. Though unlikely, Fiji had strict refund laws surrounding services to tourists. A lawsuit was an easy thing to bring if the family wanted their money back or a reduced fee and Mark didn't provide it.

Besides, finding missing people, even on a small island, was a lot of work. He enjoyed waking up at ten and leaving work at three every day.

"I'll tell you what, Ms. Gilmore, I'll think about it."

"What's there to think about? I'll pay your fee."

"I know, but it's just a matter of whether or not I want to take the case. Give me a day to sleep on it, will ya?"

"Sure." She stuffed her phone back into her purse. "My brother's probably dead in some ditch, and you want time to think about it."

Mark kept quiet as she rose, said "thank you" curtly, and stormed out of the office.

4

The crackle of lightning startled Mark as he walked out of his building. Storms, though infrequent, appeared out of nowhere, pouring over the island in anger then disappearing.

Massive rain droplets crashed into the pavement and the trees. Mark lifted his collar and trotted to his car. The home, tucked neatly on a hill between other massive houses, was no more than ten miles away. Something they called McMansions back in Los Angeles.

He parked about a hundred feet from the house. There were no gates here. Back in L.A., a home like this, with all the luxuries sitting around inside, would be gated off with night security around. But here, there was little to fear from people. The biggest dangers were the undertow and the mosquitoes.

Hiking up the winding driveway, a folder tucked under his arm, the amount of space struck him. The mansion probably contained nine or so bedrooms. Nine bedrooms for a middle-aged couple with no kids. While back in town, in what was considered the slums of the city —though really, even the slums were better than many nicer parts of other cities—people crammed into tenements. Five or ten at a time in a one-bedroom tenement.

Mark noticed a deep gold trim at the tops of the porch's Corinthian columns. He looked to them as he knocked on the door. A woman wearing white, almost see-through pants and a white top with a tan belt answered. She was holding a wine glass filled with an amber drink.

"Mark," she said with a hint of surprise in her voice. "I wasn't expecting you."

"No, sorry. I shoulda called first. But I thought I would just pop in and see if you were here."

"You're getting soaked, poor thing. Come in."

The interior of the home was even more impressive. A mixture of glass, black and white furniture, expensive paintings, and a staircase with no railing leading to the second floor. The artwork was not in Mark's usual sphere. He didn't recognize them but somehow knew they were originals and worth a heck of a lot more than he would probably ever make in his life.

"It's about your husband, Callie."

"Did you find something?" She sat down on the couch.

He got the impression he was supposed to sit next to her but opted instead to sit on the leather recliner next to a glass coffee table. "I did. I'm afraid your suspicions were correct." He pulled out the folder and laid several photos on the coffee table. Her husband kissing his mistress, her husband grabbing her butt as they entered a store, her husband walking into a hotel with her. "Sorry, Callie. I know this is hard to take."

She sipped the wine then sighed. "No, no it was expected. He's an ass. And this isn't the first time. I'm preparing for a divorce. I'm just waiting to get back to Connecticut, and I'll file first. This is just additional... whatever."

"Oh. Well, I'm sorry just the same."

She sipped her wine again, her gaze glued to him. He grew uncomfortable and decided it was time to leave.

"I'll email you the reports and the photos today. If you need anything else, please don't hesitate to get in touch with me."

"You're leaving? Stay a little bit. Join me for a glass of wine."

"I gotta get back to the city. Have some things to catch up on." He rose. "Again, call me if you need anything."

"Mark?" She placed her hand on his arm. "I would really like if you stayed. Not as part of the job. Just as a... friend."

"Um... I better not. I really do have to get back."

Her face lost the softness of just a moment ago. Her lips turned to straight lines, and her eyes narrowed. "Fine. Go."

At the door, he heard her say something but didn't stay to find out what. Callie didn't strike him as a woman that was used to rejection, and he didn't know how she would react. Probably not pay her bill, at the least. He had to change tactics and start taking payments up front.

As he walked to the car, another vehicle came up the driveway. Callie's husband, Richard. He stopped his black Mercedes and rolled down the window. Mark kept his head down and kept walking. Hoping he could just slide by.

"Excuse me," Richard said. "Do I know you?"

"No."

"Hey, wait a second, I'm talking to you. What're you doing at my house?"

"I think you and your wife should have a talk, Mr.

Donavan."

The driveway wasn't large enough for the car to turn around, and Richard didn't get out of the car. Once at his own car, Mark glanced back at the house. Richard watched him from the front porch.

Mark couldn't decide which of them he felt sorrier for.

Mark spent the rest of the day lounging on the beach. He soaked up as much sun as he could, as he did most days. So much that he was probably permanently brown now. Many of the fishermen had the same skin color, a dark brown that was almost orange. But the salt and wind of a lifetime on the ocean had also shaped their skin into a leathery texture.

As evening fell, Mark sipped a beer and ate a light dinner of rice and curry chicken. Maybe a few hundred yards down the beach, the party kicked into gear. Some red and white banners were up declaring a welcome to the oil executive, and a live band was there, playing, of all things, reggae music. The crowd was growing larger, particularly at the two open bars on either side of the party.

Mark debated going down. He was in the middle of a good book, a non-fiction piece about a squad of Marines stranded on a Japanese island during the Second World War. But the book could wait. Besides, reading put him to sleep after a short while, and he preferred doing it at night.

He ambled up the beach, his gaze on the sea. The waves rolled and crackled against the shore, and a boat floated a few hundred yards out. The engine hummed along, and soon it melted into the background with the waves. He only noticed it again when it stopped and the boat seemed to idle. He couldn't see anyone on it. The boat just drifted with the current. Nothing unusual, as many people stopped their boats out there to eat or relax or for more intimate activities. He ignored it and kept going.

The party probably boasted about a thousand people already. Mark made his way through the crowd to the bar. "Jack and Coke, please," he said to the bartender, a native islander in white clothing with a red bowtie. He gave him his drink, and Mark left him a tip in a large wine glass on the bar.

Four years wasn't a long time to live on this island, but in that time, Mark had gotten to know just about everybody. He saw members of the provincial council, the equivalent of state legislators back in the States; he saw commissioners, chiefs and senators. All of them were mingling and shaking hands, with large, fake smiles on their faces. No matter where you were in the world, politicians were all the same.

Someone lit tiki torches as night fell. The moon ignited the ocean a dull white. Mark was standing by himself near the water staring at it, the crowds growing larger and drunker behind him.

Someone else had broken away from the crowds and was sitting in the sand. Riki Gilmore.

Her arms rested on her knees, and a beer dangled from her fingers. She glued her gaze to the ocean, but in the light of the torches, Mark could see deep contemplation filled her eyes. She appeared so lonely and vulnerable that Mark wondered if, on top of her missing brother, something else had happened as well.

"I never really saw the stars until I moved out here," he said, walking up to her.

She looked to him then back at the ocean. "It's a beautiful place to live. I can see why my brother chose to come here every year."

"It's right on that cusp that places like this eventually get to. Enough people know about it to have a good tourist economy, but it's exclusive enough that it won't become Disneyland. At least for a while."

"I like Disneyland," she said sullenly. She blinked as though clearing away a thought and said, "I'm sorry for being angry with you today. It's just..."

"No apology necessary." He sat down next to her.

"My father was an alcoholic. He left us when we were young, and my mother slowly started withdrawing after that. I was the oldest, so I raised everyone. I feel responsible for what happens to Billy."

"You know, there's a good possibility he just found a girl and ran off. It happens all the time. And then usually, months down the road, he'll give you a call letting you know he's okay."

She placed her beer bottle onto the sand. "I hope that's all it is."

They didn't speak again. Instead, they sat quietly and watched the moonlight reflect off the water, until she wordlessly rose and walked away.

5

The ocean wasn't as calm it should've been this late at night. When the yacht stopped about five hundred yards from shore, all they could see were the twinkling lights of a party. Another boat farther in drifted along without the engine on. Miguel had seen it before. It belonged to one of the island's oldest residents, Stanley something or other.

"What're you looking at?" his girlfriend, Rachel, said from somewhere behind him.

"That boat. It's just been drifting around for the past hour."

"So what?"

"I know that guy. He's never out this late. He's an older dude. I wonder if he had a heart attack or something."

"He's probably passed out drunk. Like everyone else."

"Yeah, maybe. Guy was really cool to me once. I'm gonna just swing over and check up on him."

"Babe," she said in the whiniest voice he'd ever heard, "you said there were awesome parties going on."

"There are. We'll head in in a minute. I'm just gonna go check up on him." Miguel brushed past her and hopped up to the flying bridge.

Rachel was beautiful. *No*, he thought. She was much more than beautiful. Julia Roberts was beautiful. Rachel was a knockout. One of those women that turned men into blubbering idiots. But Miguel never had trouble with women. He had discovered early that if he asked out every beautiful woman he saw, he had about a fifty-fifty shot of getting a yes. With his wealth, garnered through years of buying up distressed properties, those odds were probably somewhere around seventy or eighty percent. Or, as he liked to believe, maybe he just really was that charming.

He swung his yacht around. The choppy waves made the vessel bounce. Rachel sat in a deckchair and looked annoyed that she was enduring this. But she would get over it. They had a few more days on the island before heading off to Rome for a week. What was she going to do? Ask that he take her back to her one-bedroom apartment in San Francisco? No way. Without even realizing it, she was bound to him, and though she might complain and whine, she would ultimately do whatever he asked.

The other boat bobbed in the water. Miguel cut his engines early and drifted forward, using momentum to carry the ship forward. Slowly, he glided in front of the other vessel before casting anchor. This close to shore, the water wasn't much deeper than thirty feet.

No one was on the deck, and the lights in the cabin were off.

Miguel left the flying bridge. He was close enough to the other vessel that he could probably just hop between the two. "I'll be right back," he said to Rachel.

"Where you going?"

"On the other boat. I'm going to make sure he's okay."

"Him? What about me!"

Beauty or no, Rachel could certainly get on his nerves. She hadn't seen hardship in her life. Her looks had sailed her through school and various employments without her having to put effort in. And then she just let men take care of her. She probably saw herself as some sort of ideal woman, one that used men for whatever means she needed. But Miguel saw her for what she *actually* was. A parasite. A gorgeous, hundred-and-ten-pound parasite.

He decided right then that, after Rome, he would look for another traveling companion. He could take only so much annoying.

Miguel stood up on the port side railing and eased his way onto the old man's boat. For the past three years Miguel had been coming to the island, Stanley was always kind to him. Miguel knew about yachting, a passion he'd picked up since he'd earned his wealth a decade or so ago, but he didn't realize how little he knew until Stanley showed him the ropes. How to tie a clove hitch and a rolling hitch and what the purpose of the different knots was, for example.

Miguel stood on the bow a moment but didn't hear anything. He walked to the bridge and checked it out. Empty. Miguel took the stairs into the lower level of the boat. The space was messy, something you would expect from an old man who preferred to be alone. Crates of dynamite used for fishing lined the wall. Blow a stick, and any fish in the blast radius would float to the surface. Miguel saw it as cheating and didn't like the fact that Stanley didn't.

Empty beer cans filled the trash bin next to the unmade single bed. A few shirts and dirty jeans were thrown in random places on the floor. Miguel walked to the small bathroom. That was empty, too. The boat was abandoned.

Immediately, the worst-case scenario played in his head. *What if Stanley had fallen overboard?* The old man was probably drunk. He toppled over and just didn't have the strength or coordination to climb back into his boat.

"Shit," Miguel mumbled. He took the stairs up to the deck. He looked over to his own boat but didn't see Rachel. The hairs on his neck stood up. A chilly feeling, like a breeze. He marched over to the starboard side and said, "Rachel? Rachel, you there?"

"Yeah, I'm here," a small voice said from inside the cabin.

Miguel breathed a sigh of relief. He turned around to see if Stanley happened to leave the keys somewhere when he noticed something near the stern. The moonlight illuminated it enough so that he could see it was some kind of discoloration on the transom.

Near some metal cleats on the transom, was a large puddle. He didn't realize what it was at first. Some spilt red wine perhaps, mixed with seawater. But chunky, with little bits of what looked like meat. He bent over the puddle for a closer look. Likely red wine, he was sure of it. But when he drew close, he didn't really smell anything.

Dabbing just the tip of his finger in it, feeling its warmth, he knew what it was instantly. Blood.

He jumped up and backed away from it, his eyes scanning the sea around the boat. His first thought was that Stanley had drunkenly slipped, hit his head somewhere, and fallen over. But the blood was pulpy, not just liquid. Something was wrong with this whole thing, and he didn't want to be on this boat anymore.

He trotted over to the starboard side and hopped back onto his vessel. He ran up to the flying bridge and started the engine, the stern tucking low as he accelerated too quickly. Rachel must've been standing, because he heard a thump and she shouted, "What the hell?"

"We're going to the police, hang on."

"The police?" She stepped out onto the deck and looked up at the bridge. "For what?"

"I think Stanley's dead."

6

Mark Whittaker seldom got hangovers. So when he woke up with one sometime around noon, he knew he'd drunk too much the night before. A few beers led to a few more, which led to whiskey and then Jell-O shots. He didn't really socialize unless he was drunk, and last night he had socialized. He vaguely remembered a long conversation with a selectman about 9-11 being an inside job. The selectman was adamant that Bush and Cheney wanted 9-11 so they could declare war on whomever they wanted.

Mark didn't remember his response, but it had been something like agreeing. Though, of course, he didn't actually believe that. He'd seen government from the inside out. Covering up the biggest terrorist attack in the world and blaming it on someone else was far beyond the capacity of the U.S. government. Missing all the signs of the attack when Bin Laden had declared he would attack the United States, and not noticing several Arabian and Egyptian flying students were learning to take off and fly but not to land—that sounded more like the government he had come to know in his work.

He rinsed his mouth out with a cup of water over

the sink. The beach was clear of people with the exception of a cleaning crew picking up last night's trash. Watching them work, backbreaking labor for which they were probably paid pennies, filled him with a sense of injustice. But it wasn't injustice, not ultimately. Because if they didn't have these jobs, they would starve. Some American corporation paid the islanders a buck fifty per hour at a factory further inland. The managers there worked the poor employees six days a week for twelve hours a day. But none of them complained. Because the alternative, without any type of welfare program, was that they would fight every day to scrape together enough to feed themselves and their families.

"You just getting up?"

His nearest neighbor, Daniel, held a fizzy fruit drink in a glass bottle. Daniel's long hair reached his shoulders. He had informed Mark he'd been an investment banker until leaving the profession and retiring here. He was, though he never mentioned it, probably pretty wealthy, but he dressed like a bum. His shorts were always dirty, as were the spaces underneath his fingernails, and his shirts were all stained. Mark guessed he liked the freedom not only of leaving the world he came from but also of abandoning social norms and customs.

"Late night," Mark said.

"Yeah? Good for you. Hey, I meant to ask ya, that girl I've been seeing, she's got a sister, and they were looking for something to do this weekend. I thought the two of us could take them out on my boat for a day."

"I don't think so, Danny."

"Dude, why not? I never see you date anybody, and when it falls in your lap, you don't act on it. I would think you're gay, except you don't go out with dudes, either."

"Just not into it right now. I'm not a kid anymore anyway. Sex is work now, sometimes more than it's worth."

Daniel chuckled. "What are you, ninety years old?" He shook his head. "You're coming out with me."

"I'll think about it."

Mark looked down the beach again, and out a few hundred yards from shore was the boat he'd seen last night. He knew the boat; it belonged to an old recluse named Stanley Fischer.

"Hey, Danny, what's goin' on with Stanley's boat? It's been out there all night."

"Yeah?" Daniel glanced out there. "The whole night?"

"Yeah. I mean, it moved with the tide, but it's just been drifting there. I've never seen him do that before."

"Hmm." He took another drink. "Weird. Stanley doesn't usually stay out that long. He likes his little cabin in the jungle. You wanna go check it out?"

"I can't right now. Got a lunch date."

"Seriously? With who?"

"No one you'd know. But if it's still out there tonight, maybe we should check up on him."

"Sure thing."

Mark changed into shorts and a loose button-front shirt. He thought back to the party last night as he dressed. The island had beach parties all the time, nothing new, but this was unusual in that the selectmen had thrown it for a single man, an executive from an oil company. As far as he knew, an oil company couldn't want anything on this island, so he wondered why the selectmen decided to arrange that little shindig.

He opted to walk to a café by his house. While not in order of his sixteen-day rotation, and he'd been there just last week, it was probably his favorite of all the places to eat in the city.

The sun was bright, and he put on his sunglasses. The streets were filling with the weekend shoppers. Though they would find nothing mainstream, like a department store or Aldo's, fine retail clothing shops sold their goods at abnormally high rates. The tourists imputed value onto something only in terms of money. So if they expected to sell, they had to mark the prices way up.

But to the locals, they gave an "island discount." Something akin to about seventy percent off. Mark earned his island discount after two years, and they'd finally come around to seeing he was going to stay. One shopkeeper, a man who owned a shoe store, informed him that many *Kaivalagi*, the Fijian descriptive term for anyone white, tried to make a go at living there. But island fever set in after the first year. The really strong or stubborn ones lasted two years. After that, they ran from the island and back to wherever they came from as though chased by a plague. Two years was the limit, and anyone that lasted longer than that was accepted as one of their own.

Not a single table or booth was available in the tightly packed café. The hostess, a young girl of sixteen named Ashneel, told him she would fit him in next, though several groups were waiting for a table.

He sat down with the other groups and listened to their conversations. A group of six Australians was discussing some television show he'd never heard of. Then they began talking about recipes and other upcoming trips.

Ashneel nodded to him, and he followed her, to the chagrin of everyone else waiting. She sat him at a table for two by the window. She didn't give him a menu because he didn't need one.

"The same?" she said.

"Yes, please."

Since he'd been coming here, he always ordered the pulled pork salad with extra vinegar ranch dressing. The pork was fresh, not imported. It came from a local, small hog farm, and he could taste the difference. He wondered what was in the meat back on the mainland to make it taste like an artificial imitation of the real thing.

He ate his meal with ice water. When he finished, he wiped his lips with the linen napkin then pulled out his phone. He placed it down in front of him, excitement tingling his belly, and dialed the number. She answered on the second ring.

"Hello, Mark," the soft, feminine voice said.

"Hey. How you doing?"

"Good. How's the weather in paradise?"

"About eighty-five, no clouds. How's Buffalo?"

"Still cold and gray."

"I've told you to come out anytime. My treat."

"I know. It's just hard to get away from work. And Jake would be coming with me. I don't know how comfortable that would be."

"I know. Is she there?"

"She is, hold on."

Some shuffling followed, and the quiet voice of a young girl came on the line. "Hi, Daddy."

Mark's heart sank in his chest. The pain and elation that hit him simultaneously was too much to bear. He didn't want to speak; he just wanted to enjoy this moment. But she wouldn't be there long. "Hi, baby. How are you?"

"I'm good. I got outta school yesterday. So I'm gonna

be in the second grade next year."

"Wow. I can't believe how fast you're growing up. I got that picture you sent me. I think you're gonna be taller than me."

A pause. "Daddy, when can I come out and see you?"

"Any day or time you want to, Sweetheart. You just tell me when."

"Well, Mommy says it's not good to come out by myself because I'm so little."

"I know she does." The pain was sharp and intense, a hypodermic needle slowly inserted into his chest. "I'll come out there to visit you soon. How about that?"

"Yay! That'd be fun, Daddy."

Mark choked back emotion. "I'll see you soon, baby."

"Bye, Daddy."

His wife came back on the line. "How's your BP?"

"It's fine. I'm still on that blood pressure medication and it's doing the trick. The atmosphere here doesn't have any stress. I think that was the big difference."

"Good, I'm glad to hear you're doing well."

"Can I talk to her a little more?"

"I don't think that's a good idea. It gets her excited, and then you just break her heart."

"Me? Leah, what the hell have I ever done but ask her to come out here and spend time with me? I even offered to pay for you and your asshole to come out just so I can see her."

"My asshole? He's a better provider than you ever were."

"If that were true he'd…" Mark took a deep breath and closed his eyes. He calmed himself, waiting a moment before speaking again. "I don't want to do this, Leah," he said calmly. "Can I call again tomorrow?"

"No, once a week is plenty. Goodbye, Mark."

"Yeah, bye."

He hung up and placed the phone down on the table. Tears were forming in his eyes, but he pushed them back. Growing up, his father had always told him tears were for women. That they were weak in a man, and that a man, a real man, took action. He didn't whine about his circumstances. As much as Mark tried to break the habit, as much as he tried to feel his emotions rather than shoving them deep down inside, his father's words always rang in his head and prevented it.

Instead of trying anymore, he decided to have a Jack and Coke and stare at the people passing by the café windows.

7

Deputy Chief Rashan Ali sat with his feet up on his desk. He was reading on his computer an article about the transvestite dancers in Bangkok when his secretary buzzed him.

"Yes?" Though his native tongue was Fijian Hindi, he preferred the barbarity of English. The language forcibly took whatever parts of other languages it deemed necessary and adopted them as its own.

"Mr. Miguel Arturo to see you, Chief."

"What about?"

"He says he thinks someone drowned last night. He wants to make a report."

"So send it to Dinesh."

"He's out on patrol right now."

Not likely, Ali thought. Patrol for him was stopping at a bar to have a few beers and then taking a long nap in his patrol vehicle. "Okay," he said with a sigh, closing the window on his desktop, "send him back."

Miguel was a tall man with dark, caramel skin. He wore a style of clothing Ali hadn't seen much. A white shirt embroidered with intricate patterns and shorts that seemed to flow off his body. Ali made it a point to lean a little to the side so he could see the man's beige sandals that covered his toes.

"What can I do for you, sir?" he said dryly.

"Can I sit?"

Ali motioned for him to pull out the chair. "Comfortable? Good. Now what can I do for you?"

"I need to make a report about a missing person."

"And who is this missing person?"

"A resident here. I forget his last name. His first name is Stanley. He has that old flicka you always see near the shore."

"Stanley Fischer. Yes, I know. I don't think he's missing."

"How do you know?"

"He disappears for weeks, even months at a time. No one really knows where he goes. But then he just appears again."

"Well, I guess that would make sense if his boat wasn't out on the water all night. So I went out there. Near the transom was about a gallon of blood."

"How do you know it was blood?"

Miguel's face flashed in anger that quickly disappeared. "I'm not an idiot. I know blood."

"Stanley was a fisherman. It was probably fish blood."

"I've smelled fish blood, lots of it, and this was not fish blood. Go look for yourself."

Ali rubbed the bridge of his nose. He had been planning to leave soon. His wife was out with friends and had taken the kids. He would have the whole house to himself to watch some dirty movies then relax in his backyard hammock and get drunk. "Mr. Arturo, you're talking about a man who leaves the country six or seven times a year. What exactly do you want me to do?"

"I want you to give a damn about a man that has lived

on this island for thirty years." Miguel stormed out of the open door. Ali watched him climb into a white luxury car, perhaps a Rolls Royce or something just as outlandish. He could see the woman in the passenger seat. Absolutely stunning. He wondered what he would have to do to get a woman like that. Probably win the jackpot in the island's casino.

His secretary, Helen, stood by the door with her arms folded. Anger scrunched up her face. Ali tried to ignore her as long as he could by going back to his computer, but she wouldn't leave.

"What?" he finally said.

"Do you remember when my car wasn't running? That thief Remmie wanted to charge me a month's salary to fix it. Stanley fixed it for free. He even paid for the parts he needed and wouldn't let me pay him back. My neighbor's dishwasher was broke last month, and I called Stanley and he—"

"Okay," he said, cutting her off. "Okay, just calm down. I'll look into it."

"You promise?"

"Yes, I promise. *Bhosde kay*, you would think Stanley healed lepers or something."

She smiled. "Thank you."

"Sure." He stood up and looked for his hat.

The day was a hot one, and the heat was not helping Ali's mood. The uniform of the police department consisted of long blue pants and a light blue shirt with a blue beret. He took the beret off and mopped up the sweat on his head with a handkerchief. He leaned against his patrol car, one of only three the island had, and finished a small bottle of kava. With only a third of the bottle left, he capped it, placed it on the hood of the patrol car, and headed out to the pier.

The police force's boat was a twenty-five foot Defender, an older boat donated to them by the United States Coast Guard. Ali climbed onboard. Dinesh fired up the engine from the bridge. Ali walked up behind him and didn't say anything as the boat pulled out of the slip and headed toward open sea.

"Good to see you're actually awake," Ali said.

Dinesh didn't reply. Instead, he sped the boat up a bit. "Where are we going?"

"Sama Beach."

Ali sat down on a bench bolted into the ship's bridge. It wasn't there when the Coast Guard had donated it. The chief had placed it inside himself.

Within five minutes, they were pulling into Sama Beach. Sama was almost a bay, surrounded on both sides by high cliffs. But the cliffs were wide enough apart that they never considered it a bay, and the water was still and clear. Ali went to the stern. He could see the boat, definitely Stanley's and almost out in the open ocean. "Pull up close," Ali shouted.

The Defender slowed as it approached the other vessel. Ali hung over the railing and observed the ship. Stanley didn't care much about appearances, and the ship appeared shabby, though it was probably thirty years old anyway. He was such a good mechanic that he had no need to buy anything new.

Ali grabbed a line out of a container and attached a small grappling hook to one end. He tossed it onto Stanley's boat and yanked back, the hooks catching underneath the handrail. He wrapped up the rope to a winch and turned it on, pulling the smaller boat closer.

The smaller boat inched toward the Defender. When close enough for a man to hop over, Ali stopped the winch, went up onto the transom of the Defender, and jumped onto the other boat. The first thing he did was go down the stairs to see if maybe Stanley had passed out drunk.

The cabin was empty, though the amount of useless junk Stanley had kept here impressed him. And how much he was able to drink, as evidenced by all the empty beer cans and bottles in the garbage. All the dynamite Stanley used for fishing stood out. *The damn fool probably blew himself up*, Ali thought.

He trotted up the stairs and searched the rest of the ship. When he reached the stern, he froze. A large stain of what looked like dried blood spread over the transom and the deck. But something else was there, too. He bent closer. The something else was more terrifying than the blood.

What appeared to be raw beef or chicken meat sprinkled the stain. And just by his feet, something else. Something off-white. Several of them, in fact. He picked them up. They were teeth. Human teeth. At least five of them.

"Well?" Dinesh shouted from the Defender.

"You better call the chief. I think we have a crime scene."

8

Mark was walking back from the café when he heard shouting. He stopped in his tracks and instinctively went for the firearm tucked in the holster in the small of his back. Then he stopped himself and withdrew his hand. This wasn't Los Angeles. No need for that.

One man was chasing another through the streets. The men were yelling at each other, not much more than profanity in the Fijian tongue. One of them finally got a hold of the other and tackled him to the ground. They began punching each other. One even tried strangling the other. With so few police on the island, they didn't have to fear arrest.

Mark let them brawl another half a minute. Their punches were weak, as though they didn't know how to make fists, and their squeals of anger drew a crowd. But despite their weakness, they were landing enough blows to hurt each other. Mark had seen enough.

He marched up to them, pulled the one on top off, and pushed him back so he couldn't attack the guy on the bottom again. "That's enough!"

The one standing looked surprised, and his eyes locked on Mark. The one taking punches looked surprised as well. Something wasn't right. As Mark scanned the crowd, he saw the real purpose of the brawl. Two young kids, maybe twelve, were slipping in and out from behind the crowd and reaching into people's wallets and purses. The men shouted, "*Cumba Ja!*" and took off. The boys followed.

Though tourists were the lifeblood of the island and well protected, some people didn't see it that way. They saw them as foreign invaders on their soil that deserved to be taken advantage of. Or, as in any society, some people were just assholes.

As the crowd dispersed, completely unaware they'd just been taken, Mark saw Riki sitting at the café. She was sipping tea, and her sunglasses were over her eyes. She smiled to him, shyly, then turned back to her tea.

The only thing Mark could think about when he looked at her was sadness. He couldn't relate to that. His own brothers had never meant much to him. In fact, they hadn't spoken in six years. So it was puzzling for him to watch her and know the loss of a sibling caused her melancholy.

What the hell, he thought. He didn't have a whole lot of other things on his plate right now.

Mark hopped the three-foot fence around the café's veranda and sat down across from her. On the table was a small bowl of pastries and her cell phone, with a picture of a man as the screensaver. "Okay," he said. "I'll look into your brother's case for you."

Her entire presence changed. She was no longer sitting in a slumped position with her shoulders down, her lips twisted into a frown. She lit up like a kid on Christmas. And Mark had to wonder whether the sad act was solely for his benefit or the real deal.

"Thank you," she said.

"You're welcome."

She placed her teacup back on the saucer. "So where do we start?"

"I'll need all the information you have about him. What hotel he stayed at, who he knew out here, what he liked to do on the island, the last place anyone saw him, things like that. It's just a matter of running down every lead. But you need to understand, there are no guarantees. I might not turn anything up. But I still get paid the same. Up front, by the way. Twenty-five bucks an hour, with a thousand dollar retainer."

She took out her purse and pulled out a wad of cash as thick as a book.

"No, not here. Put your money away before some pickpocket follows you to your hotel. Come to my office. My secretary will have some documents for you to fill out first."

"I really appreciate you doing this."

"Well," he said, taking one of the pastries off the plate and popping it into his mouth, "let's just hope we don't end up regretting it."

Mark sat in his office while Riki signed up. He could hear her soft voice, feminine and somewhat sultry, through the open door. She was quite attractive, though Mark had a rule that he would never get mixed up with clients again. It made for uncomfortable situations later on. Plus, they never worked out. Whenever he began dating a woman, he always thought, *What if we had kids? What would we tell them was the story of how we met?* And telling their kids they met because of the disappearance of their uncle, or because their former husband was cheating on them, or because they had a stalker they wanted followed was not the most romantic of ways to meet.

When Riki finished, she came to his door, a wide smile on her face, "Thank you again."

"No worries. I'll get in touch with you as soon as I know anything."

She stood there awkwardly a moment, unsure what to say or perhaps knowing what she wanted to say but unsure how Mark would take it. She finally said, "He... I raised him."

"I know."

She nodded then left.

Mark went out front to gather her paperwork. She'd filled out the information forms in perfect handwriting. They usually preferred to have those typewritten, but the handwriting was so clear Mark didn't need it. He wondered if she came from prep schools and expensive colleges. From money.

A streak of bitterness went through him, and he was angry. Mostly angry at himself for being bitter about something like that.

Mark had been raised in as blue-collar a neighborhood as you could get, a suburb not far from Echo Park. Most of the people in the surrounding homes were construction workers or cops. The two professions all the kids knew they'd be going into from the moment they understood what a job was and why you needed one. Some of the kids chose a third route, becoming a criminal, but that was rare. And usually those were the kids from homes with parents who couldn't have cared less what they did or where they were during the day.

Mark scanned the completed file for William Thomas Gilmore and was amazed how little information there actually was. Riki seemed to know little about anything at all. She knew which beach he was at when she called him, knew which hotel he was staying at, but that was it. She had no idea who he was spending time with out here, whether he was into drugs, or a thousand other things she should've known if the two of them were close. Something wasn't adding up about her story.

Regardless, Mark could already guess how this was going to turn out. He wouldn't find anything, she would be upset and probably ask for her money back, he would say no, and a Fijian court would decide the matter.

He regretted his decision to take this case and cursed himself for not following his gut. But she was shaken up about this, and he certainly wasn't going to sign her up and dump her the same day. He decided he'd poke around a little and see what he could find. Maybe it'd be an interesting case. Certainly better than all the cheating spouses he'd been dealing with.

9

The Bastion Hotel was a cream-colored building in the heart of Vusa. Its three flags outside represented India, Fiji, and the United States. A doorman was letting people in and out. Mark nodded to him as he held the door open. As he walked inside, he wondered whether to tip the doorman for something like that. He would Google it while he was in here and see.

The clerks, a man and woman dressed in suit coats and dark pants, stood behind the counter. He vaguely recognized the man but not the woman.

"Hi, I'm looking for some information about William Gilmore. He went by the name Billy Gilmore. I was wondering if you perhaps remembered him?"

The woman rolled her eyes and returned to whatever she was doing, but the male looked at him sternly and said, "You're with that woman, aren't you?"

"His sister? Riki?"

"I don't know who she is. But she came in here shouting and acting like a crazy person. We were thinking about calling the police."

"What was she shouting about?"

"That we were hiding something. As though I would care about some American tourist enough to hide information."

The way he said "American," Mark could almost see his revulsion. Only a sliver of the island's population shared his attitude. Without American tourists, they would all be working in factories or fishing, and most people recognized that and were grateful. But some people simply blamed the United States for all the world's ills, whether it was true or not. People just needed someone to blame, and America happened to be the dominant world power right now. Mark wondered if Rome had been blamed for all the world's problems as well, or France or the British Empire. He had a feeling being on top brought many detractors.

"What happened to him, exactly?" Mark asked, ignoring the smugness.

"How should I know? He checked in one day, and the next he was gone."

"Was he staying here with anybody?"

"Yes, a woman."

Mark opened a note-taking app on his phone. "Do you remember her name?"

"I can look it up, but I won't."

He knew why. He took out his wallet and laid a ten-dollar Fijian bill on the table. The bills used to have pictures of prime ministers and queens of England, but fish, seagulls, and depictions of government buildings replaced them. "The name?" he asked.

The man looked at the ten. If he took it and gave him the name, Mark might leave and not ask any more questions. So he should ask for more. But if he asked for more, and Mark said, "Forget it," and left, he wouldn't get anything.

Finally, the man took the bill, stuffing it quickly into

his pocket before turning to his computer. Only a moment passed before he said, "Rebecca Langley."

"She still here at the hotel?"

"Yes."

"What room?"

The man stared at him blankly. Mark laid another ten on the table.

"Room 217."

"Thank you for your help." Mark jogged up the rickety stairs to the second floor. The building itself was old, but the interior was well cleaned and painted. The rugs were all spotless, and the furniture looked new. The hotel appeared like a comfortable place for a tourist to stay, but something was a little off about it. He didn't know whether it was the staff or what, but something just didn't quite sit well with him.

He knocked on Room 217's door. No answer. He tried again then stepped to the side and waited a couple of minutes. Then he dropped to his hands and knees and peered through the gap between the door and the floor. No movement inside. She wasn't here.

Back downstairs, the man was helping someone else. Mark wandered around the lobby, staring at some of the paintings up on the walls. The clerk became free a moment later, and Mark approached him. "How much to call me when she gets in?" he said. No use in circumlocution.

"Twenty," the man said. Mark laid a twenty down on the counter and wrote his phone number on it with a pen.

"I'm a private detective trying to find out why Billy Gilmore disappeared, in case you're curious."

The man shrugged as he put the money in his pocket. "Doesn't really matter to me."

10

Marlene Hallwell lay on the lounge chair, soaking in as much sun as possible. Her boy was playing out in the surf, picking up handfuls of wet sand and flinging them into the ocean as far as he could. She glanced down at him to make sure he was all right. It was still early, and most people liked to come out in the afternoon here. The sun stayed over Kalou Island seemingly forever. Last year when they were here, she remembered watching one sunset at a good fifteen minutes past ten p.m.

Timothy ambled up the beach, wiping wet sand off his palms on his shorts. He flopped down next to his mother and sighed. Marlene knew what was coming next. The cry of every ten-year-old in the world: "I'm bored." Sometimes she felt like her primary duty as a mother was to make sure her son was entertained. She didn't remember it being like this when she was a child. Back then, kids had imagination and could entertain themselves. But the world had been a different place then. You could actually let your children outside to play without too much concern about them being kidnapped or killed.

But now the world was something else entirely.

"Mom, I'm bored."

"So go swimming."

"I did. I'm still bored. There's no other kids here."

"They'll be here later. It's still morning. Go make a sandcastle or something."

"A what?"

She fumbled in the sand next to her chair until her fingers wrapped around her iPhone. "Here, play a game."

"What game?"

"Timothy, I don't know. Occupy yourself. I can't entertain you every second of every day. Go take some pictures or something to send back home to your father."

He sighed again. But he must've figured that was at least something to do, so he rose and walked off.

Timothy glanced back at his mother after a few minutes. She was still lying on the chair, tanning herself. The past four days they'd been here, that seemed like all she wanted to do. That, and go out to bars at night and leave him in the hotel room. He didn't even know why she brought him along. He thought it had something to do with an order from a judge, but he wasn't sure what that meant. Every year, he visited her for two months in the summer, and every year, they travelled around for two months. He got the impression that she didn't want to be home with him because she was scared of something. Maybe even of spending time with him. Though why she would be scared of him, he couldn't possibly understand.

He snapped a few photos of the ocean then grew bored of that. Behind them was thick jungle. He just couldn't resist the draw of the tall trees and the multi-colored plants, so he walked up to the edge of the jungle and stared inside. His mother wasn't even paying attention. He began fighting his way through the shrubbery in search of a cool picture.

The great reptile lay on the jungle floor. The soft leaves that had fallen gave it a comfortable sensation on the underside of its belly, though in reality it cared little for comfort.

Coiled around itself, it rested its massive head upon its back. It was perfectly, deathly still, something unique to its species. And though it didn't have the brain capacity to understand such a thing, it even knew how to stop its heart for several moments at a time, an evolutionary adaption that made it part of the background of any environment. Prey might just happen by without even noticing its enormous girth.

The forked tongue, its great sensor, whipped out of its mouth. More sensitive than the eyes, ears, nose, and touch of any human being, it could detect the motions, scents, the beating of its prey's heart, and even whether the prey was diseased. It knew all things instantly in one powerful burst of information whose sole purpose was to tell it whether the prey was edible or not. That was the perennial question it asked itself through its existence. The only thing that gave its life any meaning or purpose.

The tongue sensed something. It sent packets of information to a brain no larger than an apple. Warmth was nearby. Warmth, movement, and the smell of perspiration. Something was alive and coming toward it.

The predator didn't move. Its stillness was the weapon most suited to taking down prey. It would strike, its teeth tearing into flesh and bone. The more the prey struggled, the more the teeth dug in. Its backward-pointing fangs were meant for capturing prey like a bear trap and not letting go. Then it would do something so unique, nothing else in nature even resembled it.

The prey was almost near. One more whip of the tongue, and the predator knew the prey was smaller than the food it was used to but still edible.

Timothy stopped a moment and looked around. He had walked into the jungle and thought he would just turn around and walk straight back, but that hadn't worked out as he'd planned. When it was time to turn around and go back, he walked for a long time, thinking everything looked familiar. But he'd walked much farther out than in. He wondered if he had gone in a circle. Whatever he'd done, he was lost.

"Mom!" he shouted. "Mom!"

He shouted several times, but his calls went unanswered. He couldn't even hear the surf anymore, which meant he wasn't near the beach. That was the key to getting back. He had to hear the water then walk toward it. So he picked a direction and walked.

The jungle shrubbery grew thick, and the path he had been walking on narrowed. Luckily, it wasn't that late in the morning, so the sun overhead was really bright. The trees above him sometimes blocked it out and shaded him, but mostly constant sunlight bathed him. If not for that, he would be really scared. But right now, he just wanted to find his mom and not think about anything else.

As he trudged through the vegetation, the path eventually disappeared. He was now trying to walk through thick plants that wouldn't give way when he pushed on them. Having cut himself on two of them, he decided the best thing to do was to return to the path and try another direction. This wasn't leading anywhere.

After a few minutes, the path widened, and the dirt hardened so he could walk on it without having to fight. As it became easier to walk, his fear began to go away. He couldn't be that far from the beach after all. He just had to keep walking, and he was sure he'd come across the ocean again. Or maybe back to town, and then someone could go and get his mom.

He kept his head low, running his hand along the bushes on the side of the path, when he heard something. He thought it might be some plane way up in the sky. So he raised his head and looked up but saw nothing except deep blue.

The sound, something like a soft exhalation of air, or maybe air let out of a bicycle tire, grew louder. Closer. He saw only jungle. When he started walking again, the little hairs on the back of his neck stood up. He didn't know the sensation, had never felt it before, but he intuitively understood what it meant. He was in real danger, and his body had already picked it up when his mind couldn't.

He walked faster, keeping his head down. The classic childhood defense. Pretend it wasn't there and, with any luck, it would go away. Whatever it was.

Timothy picked up the pace. Once beautiful, the red and yellow flowers, the intense green leaves on the trees and the thin vines that dangled from them, now seemed dark and ominous.

"Mom!" he shouted again. But he received no reply.

He slowed a little, debating which direction to go. The sound was so close it was almost next to him. And he realized something just then. The sound wasn't following him. He had been approaching it.

A slow whisper just behind him. He froze. His stomach tightened, and warmth trickled down his legs. And something else was there on his leg. Something black and slick. It emerged from between his ankles and softly curled around his calf. The surface of the thing was smooth, almost like silk. But when it tightened, the muscle quivered beneath. And the thing kept tightening and tightening.

Timothy turned just as he heard a loud hiss and blackness took him. He knew it had pulled him into the air because he didn't feel the ground underneath him anymore. But he hadn't seen anything. Just a flash of movement, and then his body on fire.

The pain mostly centered in his back and chest. A piercing, fiery pain that shot through him so fast it astounded him. He screamed, but it was muffled.

The blackness frightened him most. No light was coming into his eyes, though they were open. A single, horrific thought entered his mind: he was inside something.

The tightening around his leg now spread to his body. Around his chest, hips, throat, and legs. It seemed like it would never stop. As if it would tighten and tighten until it simply cut through him. But he didn't have time to focus on the tightening because he was hearing another sound now. Not hearing, not really, more like feeling. A series of snaps that began in his legs and ran up through the rest of his body, accompanied by a fiery agony that nearly made him black out.

Timothy had broken his arm before when his bike crashed onto a curb. He had never heard a bone break and thought his mother was exaggerating when she told him his arm was broken.

But now he knew what that meant.

His last thought was of his mother as every bone in his body simultaneously shattered, and his heart exploded.

11

The day dragged by slowly when he had nothing to do. Mark ran a background check on Billy. Nothing out of the ordinary. A couple arrests for pot and a bad credit history for a repossessed car.

Then he ran one on Riki.

Hers was much more interesting. Not a single arrest. Her credit history didn't show a single late payment on anything. Her current address was listed in Austin, Texas. Not California as she had said. But then again, sometimes these reports were outdated.

At lunchtime, he ate at a little seaside crab shack and ordered a fish sandwich and fries to go. He dropped them off at the school and watched as Mariah gave the boy the sack lunch. He often wondered things about the boy. Who he would grow up to become, would this mean anything to him or would he not even remember, would he become a good man or a bad one?

With his own daughter, he couldn't answer such questions. He didn't know who she was. His ex kept a tight lid on her and, Mark knew, purposely limited their contact time. Leah wanted their daughter to bond with her new husband, Jake. So far, the bond hadn't formed. From what Mark could tell, which was little, the man had difficulty around children.

Mark had thought about a custody suit more times than he could count. In the end, he didn't know if he had the fight in him. Leah wouldn't give up easy, and their daughter would be on the stand during a trial, choosing between parents. But it would be much better for her to live out here. The education system was actually superior to the United States. When children left middle school here, they typically spoke three languages and had already taken two semesters of calculus.

Mark thought back to his own father, who had only graduated high school. He was one of the smartest men Mark knew. He wondered if the education system could really have declined so much in just forty years, and what would it look like forty years from now.

Well, this wasn't a time for philosophizing. He had to find something to kill some time while he waited for the phone call. As he rose to leave his office, a man in a police uniform said hello to his secretary.

Rashan Ali leaned against her desk and smiled widely as he flirted with her. As he did every time he was here. He saw Mark, said a few more words to her, laughed, and walked into the office. Mark sat back down into the chair.

"She's outta your league."

"I'm not sure what that means." He sat down and placed his hat on the desk.

"Literally or figuratively?"

"Both."

Mark smiled. In reality, most people's English was fluent on the island, and because of the dominance of American television, they even understood colloquialisms and expressions. Sometimes better than he did. "To what do I owe the pleasure?"

"I have a case the chief would like contracted to you. If you're interested."

"Actually, I am. You caught me at a bit of a slow time."

"Good. It's a missing persons."

"It's not Billy Gilmore by chance?"

"No. Stanley. The old man that was always out on his boat."

"Oh, right. The old Marine. You sure he's missing?"

"That's what I thought, too. He leaves the islands for months at a time. But we found something on his boat."

"What?"

His forehead crinkled. "You better have a look yourself."

The day was turning out to be a hot one. Mark always carried a handkerchief that he used to mop up the sweat on his forehead and neck. When no one was looking, he dried his armpits and chest with it.

He could take the heat, but the mugginess was something else. Much of the time, it felt like he was in a sauna. The sensation, other than the constant drip of sweat, wasn't entirely unpleasant, though.

Ali drove them down to the pier and parked right up on the sand, something for which anyone else would've been arrested. Out in the distance, Mark saw something he had never seen near the island. A massive ship. Sometimes cruise ships came by, but Kalou had no major ports, so they could never dock. This one was close, and it didn't look like a cruise ship. More like an oil tanker.

"What'dya think they're doin'?" Mark asked as the two men trudged through the sand.

Ali glanced to him. "You living under a rock, Mark?"

"I hear that a lot. Don't really stay up on island gossip."

"We've contracted with VN Oil. They're beginning drilling next year."

Mark stopped and turned to Ali. "You're kiddin' me?"

He shook his head. "No. It's a big deal. They're promising jobs for every man and woman on the island that wants one."

"I bet they are."

"I'm not a mind reader, but I'm guessing you don't approve."

"The island is perfect the way it is. I just don't want that ruined."

Ali shrugged. "It goes higher than us two."

They continued their walk up the beach. A wooden pier jutted out into the crystal blue waters. At the end was a small shack with a straw roof, something intended for use as a lifeguard station but used instead as a place for boaters to try to sober up before heading out if they were too drunk.

Lashed to the pier was Stanley's boat. Ali climbed aboard first, and Mark followed. The boat bobbed slightly with the swells. Mark gripped the handrail and waited until Ali answered a phone call. He spoke in Fijian. Mark picked up a few words here and there, but he was no polyglot. Language had always been difficult for him. And one of the factors that made him choose this particular island was that Wikipedia said about ninety-eight percent of the population spoke fluent English.

Ali hung up and replaced the phone in his pocket. He turned to Mark with a look on his face that said he wasn't happy with whatever news he'd just heard.

"What?" Mark asked.

"Another missing person. A mother's hysterical at the

station right now. She's saying her boy disappeared from the beach. Probably just another drowning. We get six or seven of those a year."

Mark scanned the boat. "What did you want to show me here, Rashan?"

"Over here."

They walked toward the stern. Near the transom, the deck was a different color. A stain. Mark bent down and looked at it. "This is what you wanted to show me?"

"It's blood."

"How do you know?"

"Because we found some meat and teeth with it. We took it back and sent it to Nasinu. Their police have a laboratory. They confirmed that it was blood. We didn't know what the meat was. They said it was human organ tissue. Part of the spleen and kidneys."

Mark looked over the stain again. Amazing how knowing the origin of something completely changed your perception of it. He had once heard pans being thumped in Africa and thought it odd out there. When he drew nearer, he realized it was about twenty African children thumping a dead elephant's hide. The sound, like this stain, had then taken on a completely different meaning.

"You think he was killed?"

"What else could it be?"

Mark stood up, looking over the rest of the boat. "I don't think we've had a murder since I've lived here."

"No, we haven't. The last one was a husband that killed his wife almost eight years ago. It's not good for tourism to have these things go public."

"Oh, I see. So that's why the chief wanted me. People might notice you guys working a murder but not me, huh?"

"You get paid either way. What do you care?"

"I guess I don't."

Ali sat down on the transom, his eyes on the stain. "You have worked a murder before, haven't you?"

"I helped on a few, but I wasn't a homicide detective. I was in missing persons and then property crimes."

Ali reached under his hat and scratched the top of his head. "Well, you're the best thing we've got right now. So it's yours if you want the job."

Mark shrugged. "Sure, why not? I'm not doing much else now. But this is a premium job. I'm going to have to charge double my normal hourly rate."

"Of course you are. Anything else?"

"Yeah. How 'bout a forensic unit?"

Ali grinned. "I'm afraid your wits are all you're going to have for this. If you need something sent to the lab, it comes out of your pay."

"Great."

12

When night fell, Mark was beginning to think that the hotel clerk had ripped him off. Seemed like an odd thing to do, since Mark lived on the island and could pay him a visit.

As he was debating what to do, his cell phone vibrated with a text message. All it said was, *She's here now.*

Mark decided to walk to the hotel. The night air was pleasant, and plenty of people were out. He enjoyed crowd watching here. As he strolled up the street, he glanced into shops and restaurants, observing the way people acted while on vacation, and wondered if they acted that way at home as well.

At the well-lit hotel, he saw a group of tourists drunk on the corner. They were speaking a language he didn't recognize, something that sounded close to Russian. He smiled to them and walked inside the building. The same clerk was still there. It wasn't unusual for most jobs on the island to require four twelve-hour days. That seemed to be the preferred schedule, though Mark favored fewer hours in a day. The clerk nodded to him, and he nodded back before heading up the stairs.

The hallway was empty. He knocked on 217. He could hear water running, then it turned off. Footsteps and the door opened. A young woman, perhaps twenty, stood there. Blond hair with soft green eyes. She wore shorts and a white V-neck shirt.

"Rebecca Langley?" Mark asked.

"Yes? And who are you, please?"

"Oh, no need to be nervous. I'm Mark Whittaker. I'm a private investigator here on the island. I've been hired to investigate the disappearance of Billy Gilmore."

"Oh."

"I was hoping you had some information that could help me."

"Why would you think that?"

"I was told you were here on the island with him. That you two may have been an item."

She shook her head. "No, it wasn't like that."

"Well, what was it like?"

She was silent.

"Look, I'm just trying to find out what happened to him. That's all. His family is thinking the worst. His sister is the one that hired me."

"Sister? I don't think he had a sister."

"You sure about that?"

"No, but we spent a lot of time together. He mentioned his parents and a brother, but never anything about a sister."

"I'd still like to talk to you about him a little if I could."

She sighed. "Look, I'd like to help you, but I can't."

"Can't or won't?"

"No, I really can't. I signed a document saying I couldn't talk about anything relating to what's going on."

"A document? Like a non-disclosure agreement?"

"They'll fire and sue me if I say anything. So I'm sorry, I can't talk."

Mark placed his hand against the wall in the hallway, leaning his weight on it. "Who exactly did you sign a non-disclosure agreement with?"

"I've... I've already talked more than I'm comfortable with. Sorry."

She tried to shut the door, but he stopped it with his free hand. "Please, just the name of the people you signed it with. I just need someplace to start."

She hesitated then said, "VN Oil. That's all I can say. Please just leave."

Mark backed off the door and let it shut. He had a thousand questions for her, but he had a good sense of people, and she wasn't lying when she told him she had signed something. She was clearly frightened of someone.

That left one person who may have known what was going on, and Mark had a feeling she wasn't who she said she was.

He left the hotel and headed to the police station.

13

The police station, as he could've guessed, was empty. One officer, a man named Dinesh Khan, worked the night shift, but he slept more hours in a day than he was actually awake. It wasn't his fault, Mark figured. He had once seen Dinesh fall asleep while eating a meal at a restaurant and knew right then something else was going on other than laziness. Perhaps narcolepsy. But Dinesh was too stubborn to go to a doctor.

Mark drove up the main street in the city to a group of condos with small, fenced-off patios near the edge of town. He parked and found unit 12. Before he even had a chance to knock, Ali opened the door. He was dressed in sweatpants and a T-shirt, and he appeared to be getting ready for bed.

"How'd you hear me?"

"Saw your car. Come in."

The condo was clean, but not the type of cleanliness that came from vigilance. The type that came from the fact that he and his wife were never home. The kind that left a thick layer of dust on the counters.

"Beer?" Ali asked.

"Thought you were Muslim?"

"I'm Hindi. And it's not like religious rules stop

people from doing anything they want anyway."

"In that case, I'd love a beer."

Ali handed him a bottle, and they both sat on the couch. A poorly filmed show starring all Indians played on the TV. Bollywood, Mark guessed. The older generations watched all Bollywood, and the younger watched only Hollywood. A slow rift was growing between the generations. It was subtle, and it probably took a foreigner like Mark to see it, but it was there.

The beer was a brand Mark had never heard of. He took a sip. The traditional beer mixed with what tasted like spices left a tangy flavor on his tongue long after.

"So what brings you by?" Ali asked.

"A favor. I have a client that claims she's looking into the disappearance of her brother, but I don't think she is who she says she is. I ran a basic background check on her, and I'm going to do a more intensive one, but I was wondering if you could look into her as well and see if you could turn anything up."

"Sure. What's her name?"

"Riki Gilmore. At least that's what she says."

"Oh, her again. She's quite pushy, isn't she?"

"I don't know. I found her pleasant enough."

Ali chuckled. "She is pretty."

"That's not what I meant."

"Sure." Ali took another sip. He watched the television a moment. Without taking his gaze off the screen he said, "Why don't you think she is who she says she is?"

"I spoke to someone her alleged brother was here with. She said Billy had never mentioned a sister. She seemed pretty adamant that he didn't have one."

Ali shrugged. "I have three brothers. Did you know that?"

"No."

"Exactly. People don't share everything about themselves."

"I don't know. I kinda believe her."

Ali gulped down nearly a third of the bottle. "Okay, I'll check with the airport and customs and see what we can turn up."

"Appreciate it." Mark, just to be polite, took a long pull from the beer. He must've grimaced, because Ali laughed.

"You don't have to drink it. It's an acquired taste."

"I didn't want to be rude."

"It's not rude to dislike something. I have some Heineken, too. Stay and have a drink with me."

"Actually, I've got a call to make. And it's just late enough back in L.A. that I'll seem like a dick for calling, so I'd rather get this outta the way now."

"Dick?"

"Yeah, it means, like, a rude person."

"Ah. I'll keep that in mind." He raised his beer. "Well, good hunting."

Mark wanted to make the call from somewhere quiet, but he also didn't want to go home yet. He parked his car in the beach parking lot near his home. Without a cloud in the sky, the moon painted the black water a dim white. He sat down in the sand and pulled out his cell phone. After dialing a long-distance number, he waited until someone picked up before placing the phone to his ear.

"Hello?" the man said. His voice was groggy.

"Davis?"

"Who the hell is this?"

"It's Mark Whittaker."

"No shit? Mark, what the hell you doin' calling over here? You know what time it is?"

"Sorry, but if I called any later, it would've been worse. I just need a quick favor."

Davis grumbled something. This wasn't unusual, and the fact that he had left his cell phone on, though it was early morning over there, told Mark that Davis was used to doing favors. As the clerk in the LAPD Records Division, he could do a skip trace on anyone in the world. He had access to files even the subjects of the search didn't know existed.

"You know, you're not a cop anymore," Davis said.

"I know. That's why it's a favor."

He sighed. "Hold on, lemme grab a pen." After a few moments, Davis got back on the line. "Who is it?"

"She says her name's Riki Gilmore with a brother named William Thomas Gilmore. I don't think that's her real name, and I don't think William Gilmore has a sister."

"That all you got?"

"No, I got a birthday on William for May 5, 1981."

"Fine. I'll see what I can come up with."

"I'm sending you an island gift basket today."

"Better have some good rum in it."

"The best. Thanks again, bud."

Mark drove back home. As he stepped out of the car, he noticed immediately that his front door was open. The door had a problem with its lock and if he didn't shut it in just the right way, it would open. Not far, just an inch or two. But Mark distinctly remembered closing the door before he left today. He pulled out his firearm and held it low.

Pressing his back to the wall, he slid just underneath a window and poked his head up. He didn't see any lights or movement inside. He'd have to go in.

With no backdoor or other entryway, the front door was it. So he calmly slipped over and peeked in through the door's crack. Opening it a little with his left hand gave him a decent view of his living room. No one there. Nothing disturbed from what he could tell. He opened the door all the way to allow in as much moonlight as possible then stepped inside.

Mark stood still and listened. He always wondered if he could hear somebody else's breathing if he was quiet enough. He didn't hear anything but the waves behind him against the shore.

Only three more rooms—a bedroom, a bathroom, and the kitchen, were in the house. No basement or attic. Mark quietly stepped into the kitchen and turned the lights on. Empty. He poked his head into the nearby bathroom. The shower curtain was pulled all the way closed, but he didn't remember leaving it that way.

Pointing the gun in front of him, he slid the curtain back.

He saw only the tile and a crack that had been there when he'd bought the place. He snuck out of the bathroom and into the bedroom gun first. The closet had no doors, so there was nothing to check. He knelt down and checked underneath the bed. Nothing there. There was nowhere else large enough for a person to hide. He holstered his firearm.

It was possible the wind blew the door open, or that maybe he didn't shut it all the way. He'd been preoccupied with this Riki mess and could've just not paid attention. But as he left the bedroom, he noticed two clear plastic containers on the top shelf. One contained old documents he wanted to keep. Commendations from the LAPD, his diplomas, things like that. And one contained old client files. The client files were always underneath his personal stuff because they were heavier. And he hadn't looked through them in a long, long time.

The client files lay on top, something he never would've done. He was certain of that, because the weight of the client files would have crushed and wrinkled his personal files.

Someone had been in his house.

14

Mark didn't feel refreshed one bit. He'd never been a great sleeper and slept in bursts of two or three hours at a time. Until he moved to the islands, he didn't understand what people meant when they said, "Good night's sleep."

Last night he'd gotten only a couple hours. Maybe less.

As the sunlight streamed through the windows, he rose from bed and showered, leaving his gun by the sink. His mind had spun with thoughts last night. *Who would want to break into my house?* He owned nothing of value, not really, and in fact, they had taken nothing. They were searching for something they didn't find. Or maybe gathering information about him.

He dressed and put on his holster and firearm. He was about to leave the house and head for the office when his cell phone rang. It was Davis.

"This is Mark."

"How's it feel?"

"How's what feel?"

"To be woken in the middle of the night?"

"Davis, it's like nine in the morning over here."

He grumbled. "Shit. I don't care. Listen, I got your information."

"And?"

"William T. Gilmore, born San Diego, California, two siblings, all of them brothers."

"You're sure about that?"

"Hey, don't forget who you're talking to."

"I know, I shouldn't have asked. Anything on a Riki Gilmore?"

"Nope. Fake name, my friend. I mean, there are Riki Gilmores but none from San Diego with brothers named William."

Mark pressed the phone between his cheek and shoulder while he locked the door. "If you ever need a vacation, you're more than welcome to stay with me out here."

"I may take you up on that. You know, a lotta people up here are pretty jealous that you're livin' the dream in paradise."

"Well, tell them anyone and everyone is welcome. You take care, Davis. Thanks again."

"Yeah, don't worry about it."

Mark texted Riki from his car. He told her he had some important information and needed to see her right away. She texted back immediately that she would be there, almost as though she was waiting by her phone. Next, Mark called Ali.

"What can I do for you, Mark?"

"I found out the name she used was fake and that William Gilmore didn't have any sisters. She's lying."

"Well, not a crime to lie."

"I know. But would you do me a favor? Would you meet us at Shambala and just sit at the counter? Have some coffee or something, but kinda have your eye on her."

"Why?"

"Just an experiment."

"Well, I could use some tea, I guess. When?"

"Now."

"Okay, I'll be there in about fifteen minutes."

Mark took his time driving to the café. If Riki walked from her hotel, it took about twenty minutes to get to Shambala. He wanted her to be sitting down already when he arrived, so he took the long route around the city near the shore. Some girls in bikinis lounged on the deck of a boat out on the water. He remembered suddenly that he was also investigating Stanley's disappearance.

The old man would be nearly impossible to find. He was a recluse but a quite affable one when he actually talked to people. He'd become a staple of the island, and Mark had even once shared a beer with him on the beach.

Stanley liked to disappear for long periods at a time. No one knew where he went or why. No one knew whether his real name was Stanley or not. Though everyone knew him, as far as Mark understood, Stanley didn't have any friends. There was no one to interview. The only thing he could do was talk to the person that reported his disappearance and see if he could scrape together enough information to lead him in the right direction.

Shambala wasn't crowded yet, just a few people enjoying their pastries with tea, coffee, or juice, and Mark waited a couple more minutes in the car. Riki, or whatever her name was, sat by the windows. He was glad she had chosen somewhere indoors. She'd be less likely to make a scene than on the veranda.

He got out and walked inside the café. Ali, already

there, sipped his drink. He nodded to Mark, who nodded back before sauntering to Riki's table and sitting down.

"I'm glad you got in touch with me," Riki said. "I was really worried you wouldn't find anything."

"That police officer there is here for you." Mark motioned his head toward Ali. "I don't want any trouble. Do you understand? Nod if you understand."

"I don't understand. Why would—"

"This isn't the States. The police here have almost dictatorial powers. They can place you under arrest without charges and hold you for however long they want. You'll see a judge when they decide you'll see a judge. All I need to do to have you arrested is let him know. So no more lies. If I think you're lying, I'm going to leave, and he's going to arrest you and take you down to the jail. I promise you, it's not as nice as your hotel room."

The woman, her face stern and strong only a moment ago, now appeared confused, as if she didn't know whether to be frightened or to laugh at his threat. Her face settled on an expression of curiosity. Though he hadn't frightened her, he had gotten her attention.

"What is this about?" she said firmly.

"You're not Riki Gilmore. William Gilmore had no sisters. Who are you, and why did you hire me?"

She folded her arms. "I'd like to leave now. You have nothing to arrest me for."

"I bet one of your IDs says Riki Gilmore, doesn't it? Maybe even a passport. That's a very serious crime here. I hope you know some good lawyers on the island. Probably not, as there's only two of them."

She swallowed. The strength in her countenance began to fade, and Mark knew he had hit a nerve.

"What do you want?" she said quietly.

"The truth. Who are you, and why are you interested in Billy Gilmore?"

She placed her hands on the table as a server came over. "Let's order," she said.

She ordered an omelet and Mark just asked for coffee. When the server left, Mark gave her a moment to compose herself. She resembled a child caught doing something they weren't supposed to do.

"My name is Riki, but Gilmore isn't my last name. It's Howard. I'm an investigative reporter with the *L.A. Times*." She fumbled around in her purse a moment before pulling out a press badge. Mark knew it well from his time as a detective. The badge was authentic.

"What're you doing out here?"

She leaned forward, closing the distance between them, and lowered her voice. "I'm looking into a string of disappearances on this island."

"What disappearances?"

"None you'd know about. Are you aware of VN Oil's plan to drill in the middle of the jungle?"

"I've heard some about it."

"Well, I have information that they've already begun. They began a long time ago, right inside the nature preserve."

Mark shook his head. "That's ridiculous. That nature preserve is the whole reason this island exists. They've got insects and plants there that haven't even been identified yet."

"I know, but they started anyway. Some palms were greased in exchange for cooperation. And I'm talking really powerful palms with a lot of money. VN thinks they found the next Kuwait out here. Allegedly, there's a lot of oil if you can get to it. Their plan is to drill right through the island and into the bottom of the ocean."

"Why wouldn't they just set up a rig?"

"Too much attention. They've been drilling now for months, maybe longer. They don't even have the proper permits yet. You couldn't do that with a rig. So they picked the one place they knew they wouldn't be bothered. Right in the middle of one of the largest nature preserves in the world."

Mark leaned back in his seat. He already distrusted the government, so what she was saying wasn't much of a stretch. He could easily see some bureaucrats taking bribes in order for VN to begin work. But if they waited a few more months, he was sure they would've gotten their permits. "It doesn't make sense. I don't doubt some bureaucrat taking bribes, but why would VN risk it? They can just wait. They don't need the money."

She shook her head. "There's a limit to how much you can take. I don't know all the details, but they're not allowed to just take as many barrels as they want. But this way, in secret, they can not only take as much as they want, they can do it whenever they want, without paying a dime to the government."

Now that made sense, Mark thought. All they had to pay were bribes, probably elaborate bribes but a pittance compared to how much the government would collect in taxes from them otherwise. So set up a quiet operation, take as much as you can until it runs out, and move on to the next place. And in the meantime, have a small, legitimate operation to justify your presence on the island. Brilliant.

The outrage clearly written on her face just didn't exist within him. Sure, the nature preserve was nice, but ultimately, he didn't care if some oil company was drilling there.

"Let's just assume you're telling the truth. Why lie to me?"

"I don't know who I can trust. You don't understand how powerful these people are. They buy congressional elections back in the States as if they're nothing. I can't even imagine the influence they wield out here."

"And the disappearances?"

"When they began drilling, people started going missing. A lot of people. Dozens. And the oil company has been paying out claims to victim's families if they sign non-disclosure agreements and waive liability. I found out about it from a wife that lost her husband out here. He was an engineer. When he disappeared, she said two oil lawyers showed up and offered her a hundred thousand dollars not to discuss his disappearance with anyone. She took the money, but she spoke to me if I promised not to reveal her name. I thought it was just an accident or something, but when I began digging around, I found at least fifteen families that had been offered the same deal. And if they didn't take it, the company stonewalled them and threatened law suits if they discussed it with the media. They're scared of something."

Mark rolled that around in his head for a minute. People would go to any limit when money was at stake, he had no doubt about that, but this just seemed too far-fetched. The oil companies already had so much money. *Would they really lie, cheat, and cover up deaths just to get a little more?* Phrasing it like that, he'd already answered his own question.

"So who's Billy Gilmore?"

"He's a middle management guy. Not executive, but

not blue-collar, either. When I reached out to him, he was open to speaking with me. And then he just disappeared. On the beach, like I said. That part was true. He talked to me, was walking around the beach, and was never heard from again."

"Are you suggesting the company had him killed to keep him quiet?"

"I don't know. I don't know what's going on, but something." She looked to Ali. "So that's the whole story. Are you still going to have me arrested?"

"I'm not sure I totally believe you, but no, I'm not having you arrested. Besides, it's so much paperwork I doubt Rashan would do it." Mark motioned to Ali, indicating it was okay for him to go. Ali nodded, finished his cup of tea, and left the café.

"You know," she said, "I hired you to do a job. I still need that job done. I need to find out what happened to Billy Gilmore."

"I'm not sure—"

"I'll pay quadruple your normal rate. A hundred dollars an hour."

Before Mark had even processed the amount of money he could make, a single flash came to his mind. Himself in court with a lawyer, a good lawyer this time, fighting for custody of his daughter. He didn't have a choice. He could do nothing else for the amount of money she was proposing. "Okay," he said. "But I want one twenty-five an hour, plus expenses. Give me that, and I'll find out what happened to Billy Gilmore. There's no American you'll find that has more connections on this island than me."

"Okay, that's fair. What do you need from me?"

Mark left a few bills on the table for the meal. "Just no

more lying."

He walked out of the café, a gray feeling in his gut telling him this might not have been the best thing to get caught up in.

15

Steven Russert had grown up in the oil fields. Back in North Dakota, he got his first job with the oil companies when he was just eleven years old. The field workers worked non-stop for so long they dehydrated themselves. The company hired him at one dollar an hour, under the table of course, to take them water and snacks during the day. He remembered saving every one of those dollars because, one day, he would be the boss in the suit that everyone looked up to. To do that, he would have to pay for college, and his parents weren't going to do it for him.

Now, twenty years later, he was a boss, but not as high up the chain of command as he thought he would be. As he stood over the fields in Kalou's jungles, he was amazed how little that world appealed to him. He'd tried it awhile. He'd entered prep school with an eye toward Harvard, the business school preferred by most of the oil companies for which he wanted to work. But that hadn't worked out.

Steven had hated his fellow prep school students. They cared only about what people thought about them. Their appearance, their speech, their careers, who they dated and didn't date, everything in their lives focused on one goal: making sure they gave the right impression to the right people. They lived their lives second-hand. An inauthentic life wasn't a real life at all, in his estimation.

He began getting into trouble instead of coming to class. By the time he was ready to enter high school, he'd already been kicked out of two prep schools. His father, himself an oilman but one that never rose above the position of foreman, was at a loss as to why the boy wouldn't take advantage of the opportunity given to him. Steven didn't care.

He went to a regular high school and, instead of college, joined the military. He fought in the first Desert Storm and was, by all accounts, a mechanic. In fact, he had been in a reconnaissance division of the Marine Corps, something colloquially known as Force Recon, an elite squad used as a precision instrument for one purpose: to go behind enemy lines and gather intelligence by any means necessary. Though missions were considered a success if no shots were fired, killing, he soon found out, wasn't exactly discouraged.

When he left the Marines, the oil industry still called to him. Something about pulling the stuff out of the ground, the smell of it, the feel of it, and using it for energy was a passion he'd never gotten rid of. But now he had a different skill set than business. His skill set was protection.

When he'd first joined VN, he began as a middle manager, hired by another Marine who hated the Ivy League, or as he called them, "fairies" and wanted real men to help run the company. Steven hated the office environment and began asking for the more dangerous posts.

Posts in Arabia, Venezuela, Kuwait, Iraq and Yemen. He longed for the adventure that he saw when he looked to men like John Paul Getty. The Wildcats scouring the world for oil.

One day, only four weeks into his post in Baghdad, an executive for VN was traveling the various sites as part of a PR campaign to show the public that VN cared about what occurred in Iraq. While traveling in his Limo in the green zone, two policemen stopped the car and asked for identification. As the driver of the limo gathered the papers together, the policemen pulled out semi-automatic weapons and opened fire on the executive. The only other person in the limo was Steven, who threw himself on the executive, catching several rounds in his back that burrowed deep into the Kevlar vest he always wore.

Steven lay motionless, and just as he thought they would, the policemen inched closer to make sure the occupants were dead. Steven caught one of them with a round in his forehead, crumpling him to his knees. As he fell, he squeezed the trigger on his rifle, hitting the other policeman in the leg. Steven got out of the limo and held the handgun, the largest Desert Eagle he could get his hands on, and fired rounds into the man's throat then his eyes. He pulled the dead driver's body out of the limo and drove back to the hotel.

The executive hired him as head of security for operations in the Middle East. Within four years, Steven headed security for the entire company.

And though they'd had terrorist attacks, bouts of cholera, and even one disgruntled worker who came to work with a pistol to kill his direct supervisor, they had never had anything like this.

Sixteen workers on the island of VN had disappeared. Twelve were native islanders, the other four mainland employees of VN. When Steven had gotten the call to come out, he expected some sort of disease, the men probably dropping dead in the jungle somewhere and no one ever finding their bodies. He didn't think that anymore.

On a Tuesday night, he was walking back from the worksite to what was basically a tent city set up in the middle of a clearing. The jungle had been carved away, leaving only flat dirt. About a hundred tents, including a medical tent and a mess hall, were placed there. He was inspecting the camp's perimeter. He'd stationed guards every hundred feet, and he checked in with them. As he was rounding a corner and heading to the next guard, he heard something. Soft, like someone whispering to him from the darkness. He stood frozen, staring out into the darkened jungle. Something was moving in the bushes.

He didn't take his gaze from the object, though he couldn't tell at all what it was. A dark mass taking up so much space he thought his eyes were mistaken. And whatever it was reflected the moonlight. Like dark obsidian stone, a pure black. Darker than night.

And then Steven felt it.

Smoothness on his calf. He glanced down at the slick surface wrapping around his leg. He didn't recognize it at first, his mind unable to process what he was seeing. So he did the first thing he always did in that kind of situation. He attacked.

Withdrawing the Desert Eagle he now preferred, he fired directly into the slick surface twice. It withdrew into the jungle, a loud hiss accompanied by what sounded like a cat dying. Despite everything he had seen, all the combat, death, and chaos, Steven had felt the cold touch of fear. Other guards ran over, debating going into the jungle after whatever that had been, but Steven didn't allow it. They would wait until daylight. Besides, it was injured and couldn't get far.

That night was nearly three months ago, and he hadn't seen the thing again. Only the effects of its presence in the men that went missing.

Steven lifted his binoculars and scanned the oil fields. They were the smallest fields he'd ever been to, and in fact, he'd never seen oil fields on an island other than the Falkland Islands. This island was special to his company. And if it was special to the company, it was special to him.

Truth be told, he wanted nothing more than to abandon this place and pull everybody out. It gave him, for lack of a better word, the creeps.

"Sir," his assistant, Derek, said as he ran up to him, "post one hasn't called in."

"How long?"

"Six minutes late."

"Try them again."

Derek lifted a walkie-talkie to his lips. "Try them again, Hank, over."

"Roger that. One sec."

A few minutes passed in silence. Steven found silence more comfortable than small talk. But it wasn't a trait other people shared. Derek had grown accustomed to it, so he didn't attempt conversation. The two men simply stared at the surrounding jungle without speaking.

"Derek," the radio crackled, "still getting no response. Over."

"Roger that. Thanks." Derek looked to Steven but

didn't speak for a moment. "Well, what should we do, sir?"

"Send a small team to post one. Have them meet me over there."

Before Derek could respond, Steven was already jogging through the thick vegetation. He pulled out the machete strapped to his belt and hacked away the massive leaves and branches that blocked his path. He could've run around the jungle on the dirt path the company had carved out months ago, but that wasn't the quickest route. He wanted to get to post one as quickly as possible.

The posts were the most dangerous spots on the guard rotation. A good half of the disappearances occurred in one of the ten posts he had set up. The posts were all on the outskirts of the camp, and each disappearance had forced him to bring them closer and closer until they were in their present situation. Where the guards were basically in the camp itself.

One particularly dense patch of vine and leaves was giving him trouble, and Steven had to hack at it for much longer than he would've liked. When he got through, he could see post one up ahead about thirty feet. Each post was marked with a white marker so the guards would know where to rotate.

No one was there yet, so he stood by the marker. It was possible the guard had wandered off for a beer. The islanders didn't have incentive for work. They felt they didn't need much, so work seemed like a waste of time to them. VN had solved that particular problem recently. They simply provided the workers with catalogues of things they could order, should they be able to gather the money. Productivity and longevity of hours increased, but there was still an understanding that they would get away with working as little as possible, should they have the opportunity to do so.

Three men broke through the wall of green that made up the wild jungle around him, and they stood in silence as he scanned the surroundings. No sign of the guard assigned to this post. They would have to check camp then the city to see if they could locate him before jumping to any conclusions.

As Steven turned to head back to camp, he glanced down at the knee-high white post. A discoloration marred the bottom. Bending down, he could see clearly that it was blood. Blood—actual, fresh, blood—didn't look like it did in the movies. It was more black than red. The only real color in it was right at the edges of any spatters. This blood was in a spatter pattern of small droplets leading down. He wasn't a forensic analyst, but if Steven had to put money on it, he would guess something had struck the guard in a downward swing from above him.

"We're gonna need more guards," he said, standing up straight. "Hire whoever you can in town. Once they're posted, I want volunteers for a hunting party. As many as we can get. Time and a half pay."

Derek was standing just off to the side. He waited a moment before clearing his throat and saying, "Hunting for what, sir?"

"Haven't you heard, Derek? We got ourselves a damn monster stalking us."

16

Mark stopped the car in front of the old house. The home lay far enough in the jungle that it took almost half an hour of driving on bumpy dirty roads to get out here. Though he'd been on several tours of the jungle before, in general, he stayed away from it.

Riki stepped out of the passenger side. Mark had tried to tell her he worked alone, but she insisted on coming, reminding him who was paying for this investigation. Under normal circumstances, he might've just told her to find someone else, but he couldn't pass up so much money. Not when he had a chance, a real chance, to get his daughter.

"You've never been here?" Riki asked.

"No. Stanley never liked anyone up here. I only actually spent time with him once. He was fixing his boat motor, and I brought out a couple beers. We sat on the beach and talked for maybe five minutes, and that was it. When the beer was empty, he went back to the motor. He didn't enjoy other people."

"That must've been lonely," she said as they walked up the small path to the front door.

Mark looked through the front room window, but the blinds were drawn. He thought he might be able to see something out of the corners, but the only thing was a shovel leaned up against the wall.

"Well, considering he's gone, I don't think he'd mind if we picked his lock." Mark took out his lock pick kit and went to work. The kit consisted of several smooth keys and a long, thin access tool. He'd practiced a few times at home, and the ease of cracking open a lock surprised him.

The trigger in the lock popped, and the door opened. Mark glanced over to Riki, whose face bore a combination of excitement and fear. He pushed open the door and said, "Ladies first."

She grimaced and brushed past him inside the home.

The house was about as messy a place as Mark could've imagined. Garbage was piled up on the floors and overflowing from a bin in the kitchen. Crusted food pasted the few dishes spread throughout the front room. An overwhelming smell of something putrid hit them, like rotting meat wrapped in wet dog fur.

Riki covered her nose with a Sani-wipe she pulled out of her purse, but Mark just breathed through his mouth. He wasn't entirely certain what he was looking for, but if he could definitely cross Stanley off or add him to the list of missing persons, he would have one less thing to worry about. Then again, the government was paying by the hour, and he didn't want it resolved too quickly.

Riki began flipping through some files on a bookshelf. Mark crossed into the kitchen then the bedroom.

The bed was nothing but a mattress, no blanket or pillow, and the mattress was filthy. In the closet were the few items of clothing Stanley owned that weren't on his boat.

"Hey, Mark?" Riki shouted.

"Yeah?"

"I found something."

Mark hurriedly left the bedroom and returned to the front room. Riki held an open file filled with photos. Mark looked at the photos as she flipped through them. They were all of women, younger women, perhaps fifteen to twenty, and all of different nationalities in different locations. All of them were dressed scantily. None of them looked frightened, which meant they were taking the photos willingly.

"Well, I guess we figured out where Stanley would disappear to for months at a time," he said.

"Prostitutes? He lived in paradise but travelled around the world visiting prostitutes?"

Mark grinned. "You're not a man. I think that might be the dream of most men. In secret of course." He scanned the rest of the front room. "I don't think there's anything here."

She closed the file and pushed it away. "What next?"

"I have a meeting with the guy that reported Stanley's boat. I can handle that alone."

"I'd like to come."

"Why?"

"Because maybe I can help."

Mark exhaled. "Well, lunch is on you, then."

The veranda at the café was packed, but Mark spotted who he was looking for immediately. Miguel had said on the phone that he would be with the most stunning blond in the place, and he wasn't kidding. She looked like she had been ripped from the pages of any fashion magazine.

"Miguel?"

"Yes."

He held out his hand, and Miguel took it. "Mark Whittaker. Thanks for meeting me."

"No problem."

The two of them sat down, and the blond immediately began eyeing Riki. Riki had a natural beauty about her that Mark found more appealing than the plastic exaggeration of the blond. Somehow, intuitively, the blond recognized this and saw Riki as a threat. She wasn't friendly and in fact leaned away from Riki, folding her arms defensively but never taking her eyes off her.

"I know the police didn't have you fill out a witness statement," Mark said, "so why don't you just start at the beginning and tell me what you saw."

"Nothing much, really. We were out on my yacht, and I saw Stanley's boat just drifting out there. I knew Stanley from a few interactions we'd had. So I went over and hopped aboard. The swells weren't that bad. Um... then I looked around, didn't find anything, and was about to go when I saw the blood. Like a stain. It had, like, pieces of meat on it. So I went back to call the police. That's it."

"Did you see anyone around? Maybe another boat or something?"

He shook his head. "No. No one."

"When was the last time you saw Stanley?"

"Oh, man, months ago. Last time I was here. Maybe like last year."

Mark glanced over Miguel's shoulder. Two men were arguing about something, and one told the other to be quiet. Mark watched them a moment then leaned back in the seat. Miguel was a dead-end. Just someone that saw the boat after everything had already happened.

"I appreciate you meeting me," Mark said.

He shrugged. "Sorry I couldn't give you more."

"Not your fault," he said, scanning the place for a server. "Maybe he'll turn up on his own somewhere?"

17

After lunch, Mark thanked Miguel again for his time. The meal had been awkward. The blond didn't say a single word and just stared at the two of them as if they were so far beneath her, they didn't deserve her attention. Mark thought Riki would be just as combative, but she seemed completely oblivious. In fact, several times she tried to strike up polite conversation with the blond.

As they walked out of the restaurant, Mark said, "What do you think her problem was?"

"Whose?"

"The blond."

"I thought she was fine."

They leaned against his car, watching the crowds pass by as they perused the various shops. An odd rush hit him, the rush of the hunt. He had felt the same thing as a detective, and it was coming back. But instead of embracing and running with it, he tried to push it down deep inside. That was the last thing he needed, to get obsessed with a case that seemed to be going nowhere.

"Well," she said, "what now?"

"You mean you don't have any suggestions?"

"Sure I do. But you're the one with all the connections."

"I don't have any connections with VN Oil. And I'd

sure like to talk to them. Maybe we can pop into this oil field of yours and verify if it actually exists or not?"

"They wouldn't let you within a mile of that place."

"Well, they had to hire workers on the island, right? I doubt they flew in hundreds of unioned, more expensive employees from the States. So how are the islanders getting in?"

She grinned. "Only one way to find out."

Since everyone had signed non-disclosure agreements, Mark guessed few people would come out and say they were working for the oil company. But the island wasn't a massive place. People held the same jobs for their lifetime. Friends and relatives would know if they were working somewhere new, and maybe *they* didn't sign non-disclosure agreements.

The bar, the type of place locals went when they didn't want to go home after work, was packed. The tables were raucous as locals downed beer after beer, and the tourists drank fruity drinks with umbrellas.

Four men sat at a table in the far corner. They were drinking in silence, each of them focusing on their own booze and occasionally looking around the bar. They appeared sullen and agitated. Mark knew them. Two were unemployed and the other two held part-time jobs as house painters. When he scanned them, he noticed something clipped to one of their belts. An ID badge. Mark was too far away to read it, but he was pretty certain the man had been unemployed for a while.

He and Riki sat at the bar and ordered two beers. "What's the plan?" Riki asked.

"That man there is unemployed. I'm almost certain of it. But he's got an ID badge on his belt. I think I'd like to chat with them a minute. After they've had a few more drinks. If they're not responsive, I can always pop into their home and speak to their wives."

Riki looked over the men. Mark watched her as she did so. She didn't look anything like his ex, which by itself made her more alluring.

Mark's divorce had been so bitter that it scarred them both for life. For months afterward, they couldn't speak to each other. When an issue arose, they resolved it by text message, because the sound of the other person's voice was too much. Eventually, they realized they would have to interact with each other because of their daughter. But those scars remained. The keloid built up and up, so thick they could never hide or remove it.

"Can I ask you something?" Riki said. "Why here?"

"Kalou?"

"Yeah."

"It's about as far as you can get from a major city. The lifestyle is completely laid back. Crime is almost non-existent. Money, except for bribes and the tourists, really isn't that important. The politicians are still crazy, but politicians are crazy everywhere. I feel at peace here. Like the world just makes more sense."

"I could see that. A neighbor of mine had their house broken into a few months ago. And I'm not rich, but I don't live in the projects, either. So someone breaks into their house and robs them when they weren't home. Well, they ended up arresting the guy when he tried to pawn some of her stuff. Turns out the guy was a serial rapist. He was breaking into people's houses and raping the wives while he tied up the husbands and made them watch. That's what he had planned for my neighbors, but he didn't realize they weren't home. They were visiting relatives in San Francisco. This happened in a good neighborhood. I think L.A. is like that. No one's safe."

"Everywhere is like that." He took a sip of his beer. The four men rose and walked out. Mark set his beer down. "Wait here," he said and followed them out.

Mark had seen the one with the ID badge several times before. He'd asked Mark if he had any odd jobs he could do. Mark once had him clean his rain gutters. They didn't really need cleaning, but Mark could tell the man was too proud to take a handout. So Mark had him do some work before giving him some cash.

"Hey," Mark said, "um, Dil, right?"

"Yes." The man grinned. "How are you, Mark?"

"Good. Listen, I had kind of a request. I've heard some people have been picking up good work farther inland. Something to do with the oil company, and, well, I'm interested in applying. How would I do that?"

"You want to work for VN?"

Mark nodded. "I don't have a lot of clients right now. It'd be some good supplemental income."

The man glanced back to the other three men, who were piling into a single car. "You don't want to work there," he said quietly. "Find somewhere else."

"I've heard the pay is great."

"It is. But it's not worth it. Believe me, find somewhere else."

"Let's say there is nowhere else. How would I go about applying?"

The man was quiet a moment, understanding he wasn't going to sway Mark from what he wanted. "There's a man in town hiring. His name is Tom. I don't know his last name. He's staying at the Venetian Suites. You just need to ask for him."

"Tom at the Venetian Suites? Okay, I really appreciate that, Dil. You have yourself a good night."

The man didn't say anything as he headed to the car. He climbed into the back and the car pulled away, disappearing farther down the road.

Mark checked the clock on his phone. Now was as good a time as any.

18

The Venetian Suites, consisting of buildings spread out over a five-acre lot, were probably the nicest rooms on the entire island. Each unit was a separate home from every other unit. The homes were far enough away that residents couldn't hear their neighbors but close enough to provide a sense that they weren't completely alone in the jungle.

Mark had been there once before. He didn't rent a room, just had a look around because he'd heard about its luxury. He remembered staring at the homes and seeing the couples inside and wondering why he wasn't in one of those.

It was a brief flash of the way he used to think. As a beat cop and then a detective, he saw fancy homes, and jealousy wrung his guts. The fact that he risked his life every day for a pittance and people trading stocks made a hundred times what he did weighed heavily on him. On every cop.

Then he moved to the island, and all that faded away. Everyone was treated relatively equally, whether they lived in a shack on the beach or a mansion hidden away in the jungle. Only now, standing at these suites, did the old envy claw its way out again. He tried to push it from his mind as he walked to the administration building.

A front desk clerk in a suit busied himself on a computer. He was staring at the screen as if it was upsetting him.

"Hi," Mark said. "I'm, ah, looking for Tom."

The man glanced up from his computer. "Do you have an appointment with him?"

"No, um... no, I wasn't told I needed one."

The man sighed. "Well, have a seat, and I will call him and let him know you are here."

Mark sat in a plush chair against the wall. The side table next to him looked like something made hundreds of years ago. Vivid, bright artwork decorated the walls. Even the armrests of the chair he sat in had been cleaned. No detail escaped them.

The man picked up a phone and said, "Sorry to bother you, but you have another one waiting to speak with you... okay." The man hung up. "You can go in now," he shouted.

"Which room again?"

"Down the hall to your left." The man didn't raise his eyes from the screen.

The hotel's typical patrons did not use the narrow hallway. It almost appeared cordoned off, as if they didn't want anyone back there. The doors all had thick locks, and the carpets appeared brand new.

Mark continued down the hallway until he reached an open door. A man was sitting on a bed with a laptop open in front of him. He looked up when he saw Mark. "Come in and shut the door behind you, please."

Mark did as instructed.

"Have a seat," the man said.

A chair sat about three feet in front of the man. Mark

sat down and crossed his legs, placing his interlaced fingers on his knee. It was about the most professional pose he could pull. He thought it appeared both interested, formal, and relaxed at the same time, though he felt none of those things.

"Have you previously filled out an application?"

"No."

"Any experience in the oil industry or security?"

"No. I worked for five summers at a quarry by my house, though."

"Quarry's not an oil field."

"No, sir," he said. "Quarry's much harder."

A brief flash of something between anger and confusion appeared on his face, then it faded away, and the man chuckled. "Good one." He set the papers in his hand down and leaned back, staring Mark in the eyes. "Why do you want to work here?"

"Supplemental income," Mark lied. "Times are tough all over, and it seems like a good company."

"Okay," the man said. "First, tell me what headhunter asked you here."

"Um, no headhunter. It was a personal referral."

The man was quiet a moment. "Personal referral?" He reached for his phone and typed something. "Personal referral from who? All of our employees sign non-disclosure agreements."

"Yeah, I know. But—"

Just then, the door behind him opened, and two men stepped through. Both wore tight shirts that showed off their muscles. Though it was night, wrap-around Ray-Ban sunglasses dangled from their necks. Both were chewing gum like horses chewed hay, which would have been comical if not for the pistols in their shoulder holsters.

"I'm going to ask you again," the man said, "personal referral from who?"

Mark looked from the two men to the man on the bed. He had overplayed his hand. He should have done more digging around before coming here. Some research. Instead of preparing properly, he had rushed in like an amateur, and he wasn't sure why.

"Listen, fellas..." The two men were much bigger than he was and could clearly take him in a scrap. His only chance was surprise then run like hell.

Mark leapt from the bed and swung wildly with a haymaker. He connected with one of the men's jaw and sent him stumbling back. Mark ran for the door, hoping to avoid the second man altogether. But the big man wrapped his arm around him as if grabbing a baby.

Tightness gripped his chest, as though his organs were being compacted. The big man had him in a bear hug. Mark's lower back was on fire. He leaned his head back then thrust it forward, butting his forehead into the man's nose. The man's grip didn't loosen.

Damn, that sure as hell works in the movies.

The other man had recovered and pulled something out of his waistband. It was a sap, short, thick, and black. Mark didn't even see him swing. He just felt a *thwap* behind his ear, and he was down.

The air was cool, a sea breeze scented with brine and wet sand. Mark had loved that smell as a kid. Growing up in an apartment near the beach in L.A., he remembered cutting school and going down to shoot crabs with a BB gun. They would swarm the beaches, hundreds of them, like an invading red army. He would pretend he was defending his city. The BBs never really did anything other than occasionally annoying them enough to flee in some other direction.

He thought of those crabs as his eyes flicked open. Above him, a fan twirled lightly from a gray ceiling. He saw a table with a man at it. The man was rough looking, with scruff on his face and a thick hunting knife in his hand. He was whittling a good size chunk of wood into the shape of what appeared to be a stake.

"Didn't know there were any vampires on the island," Mark said, sitting up with a groan. His vision still wasn't stable, and he felt dizzy. He closed his eyes a moment then opened them again, taking in the room.

"Not for vampires, brother."

The man was about Mark's size, not like the gargantuan that had knocked him out and stuck him here, but something about the man was menacing. The calm, maybe. He was in a stressful situation for both parties, but the man remained perfectly calm. Like he was lying on the beach soaking in the sun.

"What exactly did I do to deserve such attention?" Mark tried to stand. His knees nearly buckled. He might have had a concussion, so he chose to sit.

"You upset my employee. You see, he doesn't know who you are, and you came in and lied to him. That's not good."

"I wasn't lying. I was referred here."

The man shook his head. "If you were, then I need to know the name of the person stupid enough to refer you here."

"I can't give that to you."

The man wagged the stake at him. "See, now that's what I thought you would say. Hence, the stake."

"You gonna stick it in my heart?"

"Nah, no real pain there. The real pain is in your hands, feet, and tongue. Most nerve centers you have in your body. More even than your cock." He leaned back in the chair and continued sharpening the stake.

"Why not just use the knife?" Mark said matter-of-factly, as though this were the most normal conversation in the world.

"Knife is smooth, it pierces. The wood, no matter how sharp I get it, is gonna leave splinters. It fragments, catches more of the nerves."

Mark closed his eyes again against a bout of vertigo and nausea. A blow to the head could easily kill a person. It wasn't just a simple thing. He needed a hospital. The only way out of the room was a door behind the man, but Mark wasn't anywhere near well enough to attempt that.

"Well," Mark said, "you must want something in order to not do that. So what is it?"

"Perceptive." The man laid the stake down then rose and paced the room. "Why did you apply for our company?"

"The dental insurance."

He smirked. "I like you, brother. But I need a real answer."

They already knew who he was. He wondered how long he'd been out, then he reached back and felt for his wallet. It was gone. "All I did was walk into a hotel room and say I wanted a job. What law exactly did I break?"

"Well, the thing is, we looked up your background. See, my bosses think you're a spy, but I don't think so."

"Spy? For what?"

"Corporate spy. One of VN's competitors."

"What?" Mark chuckled. "That's ridiculous."

"I know. Especially since we picked up that little filly of yours, and she told us you were a private investigator."

The two men looked at each other in silence.

"Who are you?" Mark asked.

"Steven Russert. I'm in charge of security for VN on the island." He shifted around, letting his legs dangle over the edge of the desk. "So, Marky Mark, what was it exactly you were investigating?"

"Is Riki all right?"

"Of course. We're not barbarians."

Mark exhaled loudly. "I'm an American citizen. An American company is not going to murder an American citizen for asking for a job. So cut the bullshit and let me outta here."

Steven grinned. "I used to think like that. That there were countries and laws. Doesn't work like that. Certain people and companies, a very select few, right around two-and-a-half percent of the world's population, run the show. The law doesn't apply to them. So please tell me what I ask. You seem like a nice guy, and I don't want to hurt you."

"Do your best."

Steven didn't move for a moment, and then he chuckled. He hopped off the table and opened the door. "You're free to go."

Mark rose, using the wall behind him for balance. He had called the man's bluff and won. As he stumbled out the door, hoping he had enough in him to drive to the hospital, he said, "What is this all about? Really?"

"What else? Money."

19

The jungle here was denser than anywhere Eli George had been. And he'd been to 'em all.

In Cambodia, he had been trapped in a jungle that didn't seem to be part of the same planet. The shrubbery closed in so he couldn't even see where he was going. He'd been on a security detail there as part of some diplomat's efforts to up his profile in the country by going on expeditions. Probably to seem manlier, Eli thought. Manlier with ten fully armed guards at all times.

The jungle in Cambodia was the worst place he'd ever been sent. Worse than the Sahara, worse than Afghanistan or Fallujah or Siberia. He thought that until he came to this place. A serene little island in Fiji that he thought would be like a vacation. The island itself, the cities and the beaches at least, were the best he'd visited. But the jungle kept him up at night. This damned jungle that never seemed to end.

He patrolled with two other men, each of them spaced out about three feet, just enough that they could barely see each other. Any more than that, and the vegetation would swallow them up.

"You ever worked for an oil company before?" someone named Donovan shouted from somewhere next to him.

"Yes," Eli said.

"Oh, yeah? Which one?"

Eli wished he could shut the man up. Donovan had been flapping his gums the entire time they'd been out on patrol. The third man, a native islander, hadn't spoken a single word. Eli didn't even know if he spoke English.

When Eli didn't respond, Donovan said again, "So which one you work at?"

Eli sighed. "All of 'em."

"All of them? No shit. How long you been with the company?"

The company. Shit. That's all these fools ever talk about.

The company was nothing more than a conglomeration run by two thirty-year-old punks who'd gotten lucky. They had landed the right security contracts and grown into one of the premiere security services providers in the world. That wasn't how they made their real money, though. He'd seen it himself. The real money was in guns. Forget drugs, forget prostitutes, the real dealers were in guns.

A decent rifle would bring ten times as much profit as any drug in a war zone. And thirty or forty times the investment in prostitutes. And the company had guns. Hundreds of the thousands of them, bought dirt-cheap from the old Soviet countries that needed to raise quick cash. The security, though profitable, was likely just a front to cover the gunrunning. So Eli had no illusions of what the company truly was. The oil company that contracted them probably knew, too.

"Shut your mouth, Donovan," he growled. "We got a job to do."

Donovan was quiet a moment. "Walking around in

the jungle isn't exactly much to do. I'm just making conversation. Hey, who's that other guy that's with us?"

Eli glanced over in the man's direction and saw nothing but jungle. He stopped and listened. Donovan's footsteps circled around him and to the front, but his were the only ones. The other man was either standing perfectly still or wasn't near them anymore.

"Hey," Eli shouted, "you there?"

"I'm here," Donovan said.

"Not you." Eli scanned the jungle. "Hey, anybody else here?"

Donovan stopped as well. Now all he heard were the buzzing of insects and the chirp of birds. Occasionally, he heard the deep hoot of a monkey deeper in. Eli lowered the rifle slung on his shoulder. *This damn jungle.* It had given him the creeps the second he walked into it. The rumors didn't help. Men disappeared in an instant, taken by things no one ever saw. Black things that hid in dark places.

Eli had seen all sorts of things in his time with the company. Sharks the size of boats, spiders the size of dinner plates, birds that could carry off small children, but something about this damned jungle unnerved him. And the more it unnerved him, the more the fear grew in his belly.

"Um..." Donovan said. "I don't think he's there."

"Hey!" Eli barked. "Yo. You there, man?"

No response. Holding the rifle in front of him, Eli walked as quietly as he could. The jungle floor wasn't meant to be quiet, though. It crunched with twigs and leaves, fallen branches, and other muck he didn't want to look at.

As he neared where the man should've been, he

brushed aside vegetation with his hand. Nothing. The damned fool had probably gone back or gotten lost, Eli told himself. Nothing more. It was easy to get lost out here.

Eli took a step back. Their patrol took them out about a half mile from camp, then they looped south to meet another patrol. The two then worked backward through the jungle they'd just covered. The patrols went on like this day and night, effectively ensuring that somebody monitored every inch of the perimeter of the camp at least every ten to twenty minutes. It would be difficult for something large to get through without someone seeing it.

As Eli turned away to meet up with Donovan, he spotted something on the jungle floor. He thought it was a pile of mud at first, mud with discolored debris in it. As his eyes focused, he saw it wasn't that at all.

Two gray hiking boots lay flat on the ground. The discoloration spattered the shoes. He didn't need to get any closer to know it was blood. He'd seen it fresh out of a body many, many times.

Eli first thought that the man had taken off his shoes because he'd sustained a leg injury then gotten lost in the jungle. The probability of those events taking place at the same time was astronomical. Odd how the mind did everything it could to explain things away as innocuously as possible.

Eli knew that wasn't what happened. Something had ripped the man away so quickly, the force knocked his boots off. A car was the only thing he'd ever seen able to do that.

Something was out there with them.

"Hey, Donovan."

"Yeah."

"Where you at?"

"Maybe twenty feet away. What do you see?"

"We gotta head back, man." Eli searched the jungle around him. The vegetation was so thick, it pressed in on him. Like thick green walls slowly closing in on all sides. "We ain't finishin' the patrol, man."

Eli gripped his rifle tightly as he backed away. A trail had been cut out around the camp so the patrols didn't have to create their own each shift. Eli backtracked to the trail and began trudging to camp when he realized he couldn't hear Donovan's footsteps.

"Donovan, you there, man?" He stopped and scratched his head. This damned heat made his skin itch as if thousands of needles poked him all at once. "Donovan, where are you, man?"

His guts had tightened so much he felt sick. Never in his life had he felt real fear like this. When he was facing a squad of men, he knew they were men. Just men who bled and died. The darkness here was something different. He had no proof of it, but it was evil. This jungle was evil, and they had stepped inside it like sacrificial animals.

The bushes swayed faintly. He thought perhaps it was the breeze, but the breeze was blowing north. The bushes were blowing toward the south. Something was in motion behind them.

Eli lifted his rifle. He swallowed, his mouth dry as desert sand, and turned off the safety. Firmly tucking the rifle into him, he lightly touched the trigger. Automatic weapons were illegal back in the States but not here. His rifle, a modified Robinson Armament XCR, was one of the most powerful available. No doubt it could turn a living organism to paste in less than a few seconds. The problem was that it didn't help calm him down.

Something tugged on his shoulder, and he yelped. The years of grueling training, the life or death situations, the constant stress management training, it all flew out the window, and fear gripped him so completely, he felt like a kid lost in the jungle.

He spun around with the rifle and saw Donovan's smiling face.

Donovan burst out laughing as Eli took in a deep breath, his knees weak. He felt like he could faint. Donovan hunched over, laughing so hard he was gasping for breath. Eli lifted the rifle and placed the muzzle against his forehead.

"Hey, easy, big guy. Easy, it was just a joke."

Eli shoved him back with the rifle. "Shit ain't funny."

Donovan got out a few more chuckles. "Sorry, man. It was just too good an opportunity. You're so serious all the time."

"Get your ass back to—"

Eli saw only a whip of blackness, as though a cloud had sped by overhead. The blackness lunged forward then snapped up, and with it went Donovan.

Recognition hammered in his brain, the blackness a thick, slick surface that shimmered in the spackled sunlight through the jungle canopy. A head at least three feet across enveloped Donovan. It happened so quickly, Eli didn't even have time to squeeze the trigger.

The blackness lifted the man off his feet, and a loud crunch echoed through the jungle as the blackness coiled and coiled. Then the massive head spread wide, revealing a pink interior and several fangs the size of steak knives. Almost gingerly, the mouth widened and took in Donovan, starting with his head. Within a few seconds, Donovan was gone. Vanished into the gullet of whatever the blackness was.

Eli screamed and depressed the trigger. He backed up. He hit the thing several times and it squealed, the rounds taking chunks out of it, but it didn't back down. It was busy with the lump in its body that had once been a human being.

One thought kept pounding inside Eli's mind: run. Every part of him was saying, *run*. When he finally gave into it, his magazine was almost empty.

Eli was about to turn when he heard a soft hiss behind him. The blackness he had shot at was still there, its massive head resting on its body as the lump slowly slid down the length of it.

The hiss wasn't it. It was something else.

Eli turned, his mind a jumble of terror. He couldn't focus on a single thought. Nothing came to him, and he didn't know what else to do other than see what was there.

The mass of blackness took up so much jungle that he thought it was part of the jungle itself. The only reason he knew it wasn't was because it moved differently. Out of sync with the way the undergrowth was moving.

The blackness reared up with a hiss, and he could see two black eyes the size of melons. Eli couldn't breathe, or at least wasn't aware whether he was breathing or not. The creature in front of him whipped out a forked pink tongue from its mouth. The tongue touched the skin on his face. A light touch, almost gentle.

Eli looked down.

The black tail wrapped around his legs, and before he could scream or run, it coiled so quickly and so powerfully, both his legs broke as he fell face first into the dirt.

The thing kept coiling around him, immobilizing his arms and legs. It planted his face firmly into the muck, and he suffocated. His body couldn't wait for air any longer, so he inhaled and sucked dirt. It lifted him, choking and gagging, to an upright position, but his feet were off the ground. The coils looped around him. They quivered, and muscles rippled underneath. Raw power. One coil caught him under the throat and covered his mouth. Only his nose, eyes, and the top of his head were exposed.

Slowly, he became aware of his organs compressing as if being squeezed by trucks from two sides. His ribs shattered, and blood shot out of his nose and eyes. A loud snap echoed in his ears. The snap came from behind him, and he couldn't feel anything below his neck. His back had been broken.

Limbs did not respond. Neither did his voice. He could only move his eyes. Apparently, the blackness had been waiting for it. Eli lay on his back, his eyes darting around, taking in the sickening scene in front of him. It didn't feel like it was happening to him. It was so horrific that his mind couldn't accept that this was happening.

The blackness opened its prodigious mouth. It was a darker red than the other one, but much, much wider. Inside, a black hole led to a nightmare he couldn't even imagine. He tried to scream, to roll away, to stick his thumb into the creature's eye, but nothing happened. He was completely and utterly helpless.

The mouth enveloped his head first and began sucking the rest of him in.

20

Mark Whittaker stepped out into the light, but it wasn't the sun. Adjoining the room in which he'd just been interrogated was another room, much nicer with carpets and decorations on the walls, leather furniture that looked new.

Riki and a man in glasses with messy hair sat on the couch. Riki was smiling as she spoke, and it appeared they were discussing their impressions of the island and the native Fijians.

"What the hell is going on?" Mark said. "Are you okay, Riki?"

"Ok?" she said, her brow furrowing in confusion. "Why wouldn't I be okay?"

Steven brushed past Mark, a mischievous grin on his face. "I had a little fun with him. Sorry." Steven stuck the stake into a potted plant surrounded by several shards of wood just like it. "No hard feelings, brother," Steven said.

"Who are you people?"

Riki came over to him. "I heard you tried to attack their guards?"

"Well, yeah, I had to. They were about to attack me."

Steven said, "No they weren't. They were about to ask you to leave."

"Did you attack them?" Riki said.

"Yes, but I told you, they were going to attack me first. What is this about?"

"They called and asked me to come down. They said you attacked two of their guards, and they had to subdue you and you were hurt."

"But I thought—"

"No, it's not like that, Mark," Riki said. "They've offered me a position."

"What position?"

"Rather than have me write an article about what's been going on, they're having me join them. I can't mention the specifics of certain things, of course, but if what they are telling me is true... I don't know. This is going to change my life, I think."

Mark's head was throbbing, and the pain was radiating primarily in his left eye. He closed that eye then rubbed it with the back of his hand. Predictably, that did nothing for the pain. "Riki, what the hell are you talking about?"

"They're going on an expedition. And they've asked me to come along and document everything. They get final proof of anything I publish, but I'll be the only journalist along for this, Mark. This is huge."

"I don't understand. What does this have to do with the people that disappeared? And who the hell is that guy?"

Riki glanced over her shoulder to the man with glasses. "That's Craig Millard. He's a herpetologist."

"What's a herpetologist?"

The man pushed his glasses up a little higher on his nose. It was so classically nerdy and clichéd, Mark would've chuckled if his head didn't feel like a hammer was cracking it open.

"I study amphibians and reptiles. Snakes, specifically," he said.

Mark swallowed. His throat felt like sandpaper, and he hadn't really understood what the man had said. He sat down on a chair in front of him, his hand to his head.

"We better get him to the hospital," Riki said.

Steven took one of Mark's arms to help him up. Mark pulled away from him. "Don't touch me."

"Hey, brother, I'm just trying to help. You want a lift to the hospital or not?"

Mark pushed up to his feet. The room whirled. He had been so drunk before he lay on the carpet and gripped it as tightly as he could because the room was spinning out of control. He felt like that now.

Riki's hand found his arm and helped him stay on his feet. She was leading him out of the room, Steven hurrying up ahead of them and getting the door.

"What does this have to do with Billy Gilmore's disappearance?" Mark said.

She was silent a moment. "He didn't disappear, Mark. They know what happened to him."

The hospital in Kalou was much more modern than anyone visiting the islands could've guessed. Many doctors were locally trained, but many came from Europe and the United States. Physicians were completely private employees there, with no government or HMO interference whatsoever, and as a result, they were paid handsomely. Enough to buy mansions on the beach. On top of that, they received ninety days vacation time a year, full benefits, and the loveliest island in the hemisphere to call home. Many doctors, grinding away hours in the big inner cities like Chicago and Nashville, just couldn't resist.

So when Mark checked into the ER, he wasn't worried about the healthcare. What worried him was why the hell Riki was suddenly working for the same people she had told him a day ago she didn't trust.

They placed Mark in a room on the main floor. The room was clean and white, with a comfortable, adjustable bed and a flat-screen television mounted on the wall. A nurse informed him that he would be getting an MRI, and he signed a few papers in anticipation of that. Riki and Steven were there as well, and they spoke to the staff, too.

"Probably just a concussion," Steven said. "Hell, I've had dozens of those."

"Not completely reassuring." Mark turned to Riki, who was busy on her phone either texting or emailing someone. "What's going on, Riki? You hated these guys, now you're gonna work for them?"

"I didn't hate them. I just didn't trust them. I still don't. Not fully. But if what they're telling me is true, I can't pass this opportunity up."

"What opportunity is that?"

She looked to Steven who said, "Well, we have ourselves a little snake problem."

"A snake problem?" Mark said flatly.

"Yeah. See, when we began drilling, I think we disrupted the, hell, I don't even know what you'd call it. The nerd, Millard, he could explain it better, he's wandering around in the hall somewhere. He said something like we disrupted the ecosystem or something. These snakes were living here, right here in the center of the island, and they think a few of the other smaller islands surrounding us. Just living out their lives. Well, seems we might've upset that little arrangement."

"Snakes? You think the people disappearing are because of snakes?"

"Not just snakes," a voice said from the door. "*Titanoboa cerrejonensis*. The largest snake genus that's ever lived. They should be extinct, actually. By about fifty-eight million years. But here they are."

Mark picked something up in the man's voice. Giddiness, like a child. Millard looked like a hippie with the exception of the two cell phones holstered to his belt, one an iPhone and one an Android. He kept pushing up his glasses, but he didn't seem to mind. He was a thin man, wiry, and his forearms appeared hairless.

"Ancient snakes, huh?" Mark said. "Even if there is, and honestly, I don't give a shit if there's dinosaurs at the center of the island, but even if there is, what do you want with Riki? And why are you telling me this?"

Steven exhaled and sat in a chair near the bed. He put his boots up at the foot of the bed, dried flakes of mud falling off onto the clean white sheets. "Here's the thing, brother, we had the native workers sign about the scariest NDAs and contracts and whatever the hell else our legal department had them sign. But you still got them to tell you what we were doing. I need someone like that working for me. I don't get them, and they don't listen. I need an insider that's not an insider, if you get what I'm saying."

"Not interested. Especially after almost having my head cracked open."

"I'm telling you, they were not there to hurt you, just throw you out. Besides, what's the difference if you work for us or for Riki? I know she was paying you. We'll double it. Where else on this island are you gonna make that? And you don't even have to do much. Help me pick out the men from the locals, come with us and watch us kill some of these damn things, and be on your way."

Two hundred and fifty dollars an hour. Mark's head spun with the figure. If he could drag this thing out for a few weeks, that was all he needed to cover his legal fees in a custody dispute. He'd probably even have enough left over to put that additional room on the house so his daughter could have her own bedroom.

He looked to Milliard, who was staring out the window, then to Riki, who glued her gaze to his. He would talk to her later about this decision and why she was choosing to go. She didn't seem motivated by greed, and snakes certainly weren't news.

"Hunting snakes, huh? Two hundred and fifty bucks an hour?"

"That's right," Steven said.

"Okay, I'll do it. But not salary. I want a retainer of twenty-thousand dollars, and I will bill out of it every day. If it reaches zero, it has to be replenished to the full twenty-thousand."

Steven smirked as he removed his boots from the bed and stood up. He thrust out his hand, and Mark took it after only a moment's hesitation. "Brother, you got yourself a deal."

21

The hospital affair only lasted a few hours. He was cleared of any bleeding in his brain and told to take ibuprofen the next few days for headaches. If they got too bad, he was to come back immediately for another MRI.

Steven had informed him they wanted him to start right away. He had enough time to head home and pack. As Riki drove him over, he suddenly remembered that his house had been broken into. He would have to ask Steven about that little fact.

His home appeared normal, nothing really out of place, but he had a feeling he wouldn't have really remembered. He got out a duffle from the hall closet and packed. Most people that came to the island thought the proper jungle attire was to stay as comfortable and cool as possible. Hundreds of people over the years entered the jungles wearing shorts and tank tops, sandals, and whatever else they thought would keep them cool. But that was exactly the wrong way to dress in a tropical jungle.

Insects, many of which science hadn't yet discovered, were the problem. Flies that injected eggs into your nostrils, scorpions so poisonous they were called the "twenty-step scorpions" because you could only take twenty steps before you died, and, the insect that most frightened Mark, mosquitoes. Tropical mosquitoes weren't the mosquitoes in California. The ones here were large and aggressive. They carried enormously varied diseases, but the islanders accepted as fact something the Western world completely ignored: that mosquitoes carried HIV.

Scientifically, Mark had been told, it was not possible. A doctor on the island had told him mosquitoes treated the HIV virus as food. The HIV virus did not activate the enzymes that allowed certain diseases, like malaria, to exist within the mosquito undigested. The mosquito simply didn't recognize HIV and digested it. Within a day, the stomach destroyed all virus particles.

The islanders insisted that medical science was incorrect. That many mosquitoes, perhaps a new species of mosquito, did recognize the HIV virus in its blood meals and allowed it to exist undigested within the insect's body. If true, every time someone stepped into the jungle, thousands of potentially HIV-positive hypodermic needles floated around, trying to stick them. The entire thing made Mark's skin crawl.

He dressed in long pants, a long-sleeved shirt, and a hat. Any area left exposed at this point he coated down with the most powerful insect repellent he could find, a gel applied directly to the skin. To get to the skin, the mosquito would have to puncture the gelatin layer on the dermis. The gelatin was so deadly to the insect that it could kill it in less than five seconds. Mark understood that it first paralyzed the insect then stopped its heart. He didn't know how or why. All he cared about was that it worked. He'd captured some mosquitoes himself and tested it. Not a single one survived past ten seconds, and most of them died under five.

He spread the gelatin on his hands, face, neck, ears, and forehead. It was as thick and goopy as hair gel. Before leaving the house, he checked the rooms, waiting for the gelatin to dry. Riki was outside in a rental car, playing on her phone. Mark climbed into the passenger seat.

"Truth time," he said before she had a chance to put the car in reverse and pull out. "Why would you possibly want to work for them? And don't tell me a big snake is a good story. I once saw a forty-foot green anaconda in Peru. I didn't get my name in the paper."

She grinned and pulled out. "Can you think of a better way for me to expose everything they're doing than working for them?"

He smiled. "Not really, no."

"Didn't think so."

They drove on the surface streets around the city. Mark watched the tourists. They were comforting to him in a way. Maybe it was their predictability. All were looking for the same thing; some memory they could later recount to other people. The biggest industries on the island were the jungle adventure tours and anything involving sightseeing.

"Can I ask you something?" Riki said.

"Sure."

"Why are you doing all this? It couldn't just be the money."

"Actually, it is."

"Doesn't seem like you need that much to survive here."

"It's not for me, it's for a lawyer. My ex and I have a daughter. I want to fight for custody."

"Oh."

He looked out the window at a group of tourists. A man with an unbuttoned shirt and gold chains hanging from his neck had his arms around two beautiful women. "You ever married?" he asked.

"No. Just never got around to it, I guess."

"Being a reporter keeps you busy I would think. I worked closely with a few when I was back with LAPD."

"I bet even in that time everything's changed. News doesn't really exist like it used to. Even the *New York Times* is going under. Everyone gets their news from places like the *Huffington Post* and Reddit, so you can't really be a full-time reporter anymore. You just freelance and hope you make a name for yourself."

"Is that what this is about? Making a name for yourself?"

"What is that?"

Mark followed her gaze out the windshield. About twenty feet out, two men were fighting. The fists were flying wildly before Ali tackled one of the men from behind. Another man grabbed the other person involved in the fight and pulled him away, back into the crowd to disappear and avoid arrest.

"Wait here," Mark said. He stepped out of the car and rushed over to Ali. "You need any help?"

Ali had the man on his stomach and pulled out a pair of cuffs. He slapped them on the man's wrists and double locked them. "I'm fine." He lifted the man by his arms. The man appeared as if he wanted to fight but was so exhausted he didn't have anything left. In a sudden burst of strength, the man tried to break away. Mark grabbed his left arm, and Ali held on tightly to his right. They raised the man nearly off the ground as they dragged him to the police cruiser and shoved him into the backseat. The man swore and spit, kicking at the windows.

"What is that all about?" Mark asked.

"Damn oil workers. Got into a fight up there in Toucan's Bar."

"Over what?"

"The father of a man that disappeared began insulting them. He said it was their fault his son was missing. That they'd released a curse on us." Ali leaned against the car, breathing deeply.

"You okay, old man?"

Ali glanced at him and sneered. "I am getting old, Mark. This is a young man's job. We need more police out here, or I need to retire."

Mark rested against the cruiser with him. "Curse, huh?"

He spat onto the ground. "That's what he said."

"Ali, can I ask you something? You ever seen any big snakes on the island?" Technically, Mark had not yet signed any NDAs or contracts.

"What?"

"Big snakes. Like, really big snakes. You ever seen any?"

"Yeah, you've got boas deeper in. The jungles are really hot, and they like the heat. I've seen some big ones."

"Like how big?"

"What is this about, Mark?"

"You didn't hear this from me. Agreed?"

"Agreed."

"The oil company, VN, they just hired me to help them on a hunt. For giant snakes."

Ali pulled a pack of menthols out of his breast pocket and lit one, even though he was still sucking breath.

"What do they want with snakes?"

"They think there are some snakes they thought extinct that live in the center of the island and that they've disrupted their habitat or something. They think that's what's responsible for the disappearances."

He shook his head. "Stanley disappeared on the ocean. I've never seen a boa in the ocean."

"Me neither."

He puffed at his cigarette and supported his head back on the car, as though he had completely taxed every muscle. "I wouldn't believe anything they told me. Who knows what their real reason is."

"That's about what I feel. Just wondering if you've heard anything."

"Well, I mean, my mother would always tell me monsters lived in the center of the island. But that if we left them alone they would leave us alone. So no kids ever went to the center of the island. She said that's why all the cities are built on the beaches." He shrugged. "Just fairy tales they told us so we wouldn't run off."

Mark looked at Riki, who was doing something on her phone. "Let's hope so."

22

After driving to the edge of the city, Riki parked, and Mark sat in the car while she stepped outside to find a bathroom. She walked with her face buried in her phone toward some nearby shops. Mark got out of the car and sat on the hood. The jungle air this far from the ocean was hot and wet. The humidity could reach upwards of seventy percent, the highest ever recorded in the jungle allegedly over a hundred percent. Enough to soak clothing while sitting still and doing nothing.

Headlights bobbed up and down on the dirt road before they pulled onto the paved streets. The road was the only path through the jungle, but just to the center. Someone going inside would have to turn around and come out the same way, or at least that's what he'd heard. The jungle was boiling, dark, and—something Mark probably wouldn't admit to anyone else—creepy as all hell. He had never been more than half a mile in.

Two Jeeps, both a green camouflage color as if they were in Vietnam or something, rolled to a stop in front of him. Steven Russert jumped out of the lead jeep and ambled over. He didn't say anything but hopped up onto the hood of Riki's car. He looked up at the sky.

"Damn beautiful," Steven said. "Never grow old of this."

"It has its charms."

Steven smiled. "You don't trust me, do you?"

"I don't know you."

"Well, you can trust me. I don't have any ulterior motives. I want to kill some snakes and make my bosses happy. That's it."

Mark looked over at the shops to see if Riki had finished yet but didn't see her. "This must be pretty profitable to go through all this for some snakes."

"Oil, man. Ain't that much of it left in the world. The competition's gonna keep getting worse, until finally we're fighting wars openly for the last little bit left. That's where we're headed."

"Maybe." Mark leaned back on his hands. "So, let me ask you, have you seen one of these snakes?"

"Hell, I did better than that. I was almost eaten by one. It wrapped around my ankle and started going up my leg."

"How big was it?"

"It was dark, couldn't really see, but big. Really big."

Riki returned, but she didn't seem to notice the Jeeps. Her face was still down over her phone. "So what happens when you kill some of these snakes?"

"Well, we're gonna have to kill a whole lot of them. Enough so that our workers are left alone. Then when that happens, they can go back to extracting the oil underneath this island."

"And when the oil's gone?"

"When the oil's gone, the jobs will be gone, too. The island will go through a depression, and people'll starve. But it'll just go back to this size eventually."

"You're pretty calm about destroying an island."

"Hey, brother, I told you, you could trust me. I'll always be straight with you." He jumped off the car. "You ready to go?"

During the dark, bumpy drive through the jungle, Mark rode in the Jeep behind Steven's while Riki rode with him. Three natives and the herpetologist surrounded Mark. They spoke no more than five words between them and nothing to Mark. Which was just as well, because he felt like doing nothing more than mentally running through every scenario of what could go wrong. Steven seemed pretty confident that this would be a simple operation. Find the snakes and kill them. If Mark had learned anything in his life, though, it was that things never went as planned.

The road cut right through the island. Mark didn't actually know how big the island was. Wikipedia stated 806 square miles, but the sheer mass of the land had never dawned on him. 800 miles wasn't a piddly little place.

The road descended steeply, and the Jeeps rocketed down the decline. Mark strapped on his seat belt and held on to the roll bar placed overhead.

"You've never been out here?" Millard, the herpetologist, said.

Mark was about to ask how he could tell but decided he didn't really care. Instead, he tried to focus on not letting go of the roll bar as they hit a pile of rocks that sent the Jeep tipping to one side before slamming back down into its upright position.

"This is so exciting," Millard said, apparently speaking to Mark but possibly to no one. "Do you realize we're going to see a creature from the Paleocene epoch? Do you have any idea how rare that is?"

"Can't say I do."

"The Paleocene is the ten-million-year period after the extinction of the dinosaurs. The reason it's so exciting is that we have no idea what existed at the time. Think of that. We don't know what large species was on land for ten million years of the earth's history. I mean, we just have no clue. Discovering titanoboa was the first time we were given a glimpse into what lived then. And now we get to see one in person! It's enough to make me orgasm."

Mark looked to him. "Over a snake?"

Millard shook his head. "Not *a* snake, *the* snake. The biggest snake that's ever lived. And it's right here, living on this island for fifty-eight million years. It's a miracle of nature to have survived. It's counter-evolutionary to lose your limbs, but snakes used it to become one of the most successful species that's ever lived. They're amazing creatures. I actually started out studying amphibians in the Pacific Northwest, but I switched to snakes when I learned more about them. They're perfect creatures. No remorse, no pity, no sadness or fear... they have nothing but the urge to kill and reproduce. Some of them even regurgitate their meals just so they can kill again. Isn't that cool?"

Mark looked out into the piercing darkness. "That's just grand."

As they rode up a hill on the opposite side of the valley they'd just crossed, dozens of lights glimmered, spread out over a small series of hills and the valleys in between. Some of them were moving. They were electric lanterns.

The Jeeps rumbled down the road toward the encampment. They passed men on either side of the road, two of them smoking and all of them with rifles slung over their shoulders. Guards.

As they passed the first line of security, the second line came into view. A series of trenches were dug into the jungle floor like France during the First World War. The only way over the trenches was the single road over which they currently drove. Past the trenches, they arrived at the tents. These didn't look like any tents Mark had ever seen. Some were as large as houses. Between them were parked vehicles or men sitting around campfires playing cards, eating, drinking, or otherwise wasting time. Some of them gave the Jeeps cold stares, and some didn't even bother to look up.

The Jeeps parked near a particularly large tent, and Steven hopped out. He helped Riki out by grabbing her at the waist and lifting her down. A slight twinge of jealousy stung Mark, and he felt foolish for it. He had no claim to her or anyone else. Everyone was free to do as they pleased, and Steven was certainly more than welcome to court her.

Even as the words rolled through his mind, he didn't believe them. He was jealous, no two ways about it.

Steven came over and slapped his back. "Welcome to Tent City, Marky Mark."

23

The enormous tent was an administration building of sorts. Inside, Mark was expecting cots and sleeping bags. Instead, he saw desks, chairs and a television. They sat at a conference table, and a man walked in behind Steven. He was thin, with a balding head and a weaselly appearance. Not underhanded, but literally like a weasel.

"So glad you two will be joining us," he said. He placed thick reams of paper in front of them then iPads next to the paper. "These are our standard employment contracts, along with their electronic counterparts. You'll be reading and signing both tonight before we get any work started."

The man began going through what the papers contained. Mark almost immediately lost interest. He zoned out somewhere around "Failure to Disclose Pertinent Prior Statements in Any Record" and came back for a moment under "Arbitration Venues at the Discretion of the Company." Basically, he figured, the entire contract was set up to screw him in the event of a dispute. But it didn't matter, because there wouldn't be a dispute. He just wanted his money and to be on his way. They could have however much time they wanted in exchange.

The meeting must've taken two hours, and by the

end, Mark's upper back felt tight and sore. He signed the papers then the electronic copy and stretched his arms over his head. The weaselly man said, "Welcome to VN," and shook both their hands. Then he left the tent with the papers and iPads tucked under his arm.

"Who was that guy?" Mark asked Steven, who had been lying on a desk reading a book the entire time.

"From legal. Don't actually know his name. The company has more lawyers than any other type of employee except the field workers. Come on, I'll show you your tents."

Mark grabbed his single duffle out of the Jeep and followed Steven and Riki. He grabbed one of Riki's two suitcases from her, and Steven got the other.

When Steven had called it "Tent City," Mark assumed he was using hyperbole, but he wasn't. The camp was spread out like a city. The streets, just the passageways between the tents, intersected with each other in perfect harmony, and the intersections bore little signs with names. It was set up so that workers could find anyone else in the camp immediately if they needed to. Many of the workers were local Fijians, but many were not. Mark heard a plethora of languages, from what he guessed was Serbian all the way to Italian and French. They had been recruiting all over the world.

He quickened his pace until he was walking next to Riki, who was listening to Steven talk about the layout of the camp and how long it took to set up.

"This is enormous," he said.

"This is nothing. You should see the tent cities these guys had set up in Pakistan when they thought they had a good reserve there. Probably ten thousand people. There's maybe six hundred here."

"I can't believe this island has that much oil sitting underneath it to make this worthwhile."

"These guys don't waste money, Marky Mark. If they say there's oil here, there's oil here."

They looped around a large block of tents and reached two side-by-side, gray canvas with electric lanterns hanging from the doors. Steven pointed to one with his chin and said, "Yours, Marky Mark."

"My name's Mark."

"Excuse me?"

"You keep calling me Marky Mark. My name's just Mark."

"It's a compliment. I love that one song Marky Mark did. Don't be so uppity." He looked at Riki. "Next door is yours. Latrines are right over there, one to every ten tents. Toilet paper in the tents. Showers are up that way to the north and only run from six in the morning until eight, so if you want a spot, you gotta hurry. Breakfast is at 8:30 sharp in the mess hall. Just follow everyone else; you can't miss it. Any questions?"

Mark didn't say anything. He had about a million questions, such as why the hell would they need him to hunt snakes if this company could afford a setup like this, but he kept them to himself. He had a feeling he wouldn't get a straight answer anyway.

He opened the flap to his tent and stepped inside. The space was dark, and he assumed they expected him to bring the lantern in, so he did. The tent was clean, no clutter or debris. One cot in back, a hot plate up front, and nothing else. A strap dangled from the top, and he figured out he was supposed to hang his lantern from it. After doing so, Mark took a deep breath and sat on the cot. His head was still throbbing from the vicious blow he'd received, and he thought if he ever saw those two gorillas or the man sitting on the bed again, he would have more than words for them.

Finally, more than the pain, he felt the exhaustion that came with age, the kind that slowly crept up. No one saw it coming, and then one day they realized they couldn't do the things they used to do and were left asking why.

The flap opened, and Riki stepped inside. "I see yours is as luxurious as mine."

"Believe it or not, it's not the worst place I've stayed in. It's even better than some of the apartments I've had."

She sat on the ground across from him. "Quite a sight, isn't it?"

"I'm actually pretty impressed. There aren't natural clearings this big in the jungle. They had to clear this whole area, flatten it, and then set all this up. This wasn't easy. Or cheap."

"They don't care about either. Not when it comes to profits."

"So they just offered you a writing job and didn't think it was weird that you jumped on it so fast, huh?"

"Well, it did come with a salary boost."

"How much?"

"Didn't you read your contract? We're not allowed to say." She smiled.

"I never was good at fine print."

"They offered me ten thousand a week."

He whistled through his teeth. "I think I settled too quickly on a couple hundred bucks an hour." He leaned forward, elbows on his knees. "Don't you think it's weird they would offer us jobs at all? I mean, they could hire whoever the hell they wanted to hire. They don't need either of us."

"I don't know. I think they figured we were going to find out everything anyway. Or maybe Steven really did want us along, and he pushed for it. It is strange, though, I'll give you that. Can I ask you something and you promise not to get mad?"

He grinned. "Whenever anyone says that, it means they've done something rotten to me and I can't react."

"Promise first."

"Okay, I promise I won't get mad."

"I followed you around. Just before I hired you. I wanted to make sure you weren't some shyster that didn't know anything. You mad?"

He shook his head. "Only that I didn't notice you. I'm getting soft. So what'd you find out?"

"Well, I saw you drop off a sack at the elementary school. I saw you do it two days in a row. What were you dropping off?"

"Oh, that. Just a little thing I do. A favor for someone." It suddenly dawned on him that he didn't know how long he would be out here. The contract, the one section he had paid attention to on length of commitment, stated they worked six days on, two days off. The boy wouldn't be getting his lunches. Maybe he could place a call to his secretary to drop them off.

Mark knew what it was like not to have money to eat. He'd had that feeling as a youth when his father was laid off then only found work at a gas station part-time. Dinner consisted of peanut butter and government bread. One day, Mark had gotten a bag of chips at school with money he now knew his mother had scrimped and saved for. It was the first bag of chips he'd had in over a year.

After some bullies pushed him down, one of them

grabbed the bag of chips. He shoved a bunch in his mouth, laughing, then tossed the bag to another of the bullies who did the same. By the time they finished, nothing was left.

The pain Mark had felt as he stared at the empty bag on the playground was something he'd never experienced before or since. Humiliation, sadness, betrayal, and above all, rage. A rage that he couldn't control. That night, as he lay in bed, he plotted revenge on each of those boys. The meanest things he could think of.

The next day at school, he was planning what he was going to do at lunch when one of the lunch ladies approached him. She told him she had seen what the boys did and turned them into the principal. Then she took out a bag of chips from her purse and gave it to him.

All the rage dissipated as though a hole had opened somewhere on his skin and let all his emotions pour out. A single act of kindness stuck out to him in an entire childhood of pain. He wanted to give those moments to someone else.

"Mark, you okay? You spaced out on me a little."

"Sorry. Just thinking about something that happened to me a long time ago."

"What?"

"It's not important." He inhaled deeply then slapped his thighs. "So, what do you think we gotta do to get some food around here?"

24

The cot was surprisingly comfortable to sleep on. It dipped lightly like a hammock and at times felt as though it weren't touching his skin at all. Mark slept well past shower time and even breakfast. He was still soundly snoring when Riki poked her head into his tent and said, "Mark? You getting up?"

"Yeah," he grumbled. The camp, considering how many people were around, had been quiet most of the night with the exception of the Jeeps that occasionally rumbled by.

He swung his feet over the cot and rubbed his eyes then twisted his back from side to side. Riki was dressed in canvas shorts and a button-front shirt.

"What's the plan?" Mark said.

"Steven wants you to help him in selecting the hunting parties. He thinks you'll be able to tell him who's lazy and who's not."

"Considering I don't know ninety-nine percent of the people they've hired, I don't think I'll be much help."

"Well, at least act like it. Don't forget you're on the clock."

That's right, Mark thought. He hadn't remembered

they were paying him hourly through the night. The only time he wouldn't be billing them was on his days off. Hell, for two hundred fifty bucks an hour, he would skip rope for them if they wanted him to.

Mark stepped outside and took in the camp for the first time in daylight. The tents seemed to spread out for miles, like some ancient army camped out before their enemy's walls. Dense jungle surrounded them on every side. The morning fog still hung in the air like ghosts, drifting away as the sun rose.

He looked one way then the other. A small line had formed in front of the latrines. He waited behind some men speaking French. They were grizzled men, hands permanently blackened from a lifetime of labor in oil fields. Their beards were scruffy, and redness tinted their skin. Probably from too much sun or exposure to chemicals.

When his turn came, he was expecting something disgusting, but the latrines were actually clean. He urinated then found a station of disposable toothbrushes set up with toothpaste dispensers. He brushed his teeth, washed his hands with a hard, industrial soap, and went back to his tent and changed his clothes. He wore old jeans and a long sleeved shirt with a Dodgers baseball cap. He tied a black bandana around his neck then coated the exposed parts of his skin with the insect repellent.

By the time he was through, his stomach was growling, and he wondered if he could still find something to eat. He walked the opposite direction from the latrines. Steven directed a crowd of men around the camp. He appeared a natural leader, confident and strong. Steven looked like the kind of guy people wanted in charge. The kind that could make the tough calls without flinching.

Mark had always lacked that quality. He felt too soft-hearted for leadership positions like that.

"Hey," Mark said.

"*Ne sa bula*," he said with a smile. "I say it right?"

"People just say '*bula*' for hello. '*Yandra*' is good morning."

"'*Yandra*'," he mumbled a few times. "Anyway, you ready to go?"

"Sure. Where?"

"We're gonna be setting up hunting parties of four men. That seems to be the ideal number here. We'll have twelve of the four man parties out at all times, twenty-four hours a day."

Mark looked at some men dumping supplies out of Jeeps. "You want to hunt at night?"

Steven grinned and reached down to the pile of equipment. He picked up a pair of binoculars with an elastic cap attached and tossed them to Mark. It was light and sturdy.

"Night vision goggles," Steven said. "Be as bright as day."

"What exactly are we going to be hunting these things with?"

Steven lifted what looked like a black machine gun. He held it up like a trophy and said, "This here's the POF P-415 in Spec Two. It is one of the best hunting rifles ever made. Running just a little over ten thousand dollars. You ever fired one?"

"No."

"It's like coming, brother. Wait 'til you try it."

Mark stood by as Steven ordered more men around. It appeared they were gathering together the equipment the twelve teams would need then loading them into packs. They'd thought of everything to carry with them: knives, mace, an MRE, sticks of honey, canteens of water, flares, flashlights... Just about anything anyone needed for the jungle, except insect repellent.

"You got insect repellent, don't you?" Mark asked.

"We got some in the camp, yeah."

"No, you have to have it with you in the jungle, and it's gotta be constantly applied. You'll sweat it off in less than twenty minutes."

Steven wiped sweat off his forehead. "We'll get some more, then."

After the men packed up the supplies, Steven informed him they would be going to the administration tent to interview the candidates they'd selected for the hunting parties. The hunting parties were being paid time and a half with a thousand dollar bonus for every snake killed.

Mark sat in one of the cushioned chairs on a panel that consisted of him, Steven, and someone he'd never seen before. Possibly an interpreter. One man stood at the door with his hands in his pockets, staring outside the flap of the tent.

"Bring in the first one, would ya, Hank?" Steven said.

The man at the entrance came back with a local Fijian. The local was thin and older, with a wrinkled face and hands. The interpreter asked him something akin to "What experience do you have hunting?"

The man replied with, "I've been doing it since I was a child."

"What'dya think?" Steven asked.

"Never met him before," Mark said. "But he seems a little old for this, doesn't he?"

"That's what I thought. Bring in the next one, Hank."

Hours passed like this. Hank brought in one at a time, and Steven asked a few questions then said, "What'dya think?" and Mark gave his impression. Almost every time, he had no impression but felt he had to say something to justify his hourly wage.

After three hours, they had chosen ninety-six men. Enough for two twelve-person shifts in teams of four.

Though he'd spoken on almost every man, Mark had never felt so useless in his life and again questioned why in the hell they would pay him for this. Maybe it was just a bribe for his silence, but they didn't want to make it seem like a bribe. He guessed he would probably never know the real reason. But it didn't matter. As long as he had enough to fight for his daughter, he wouldn't ask too many questions.

Lunch was an enormous undertaking. The camp ate in shifts, though the majority of the workers were out in the oil fields and ate bagged meals there. A mess hall was set up complete with buffet representing every nationality of food, from Indian and Nepalese to Mexican and Greek. Mark got the impression the company wanted to do everything possible to keep their workers happy.

"Got some business to attend to," Steven said. "Catch you later."

Standing in the mess hall by himself suddenly transported Mark back to junior high school. The worst moment of lunch every day was when he'd gotten his food and had to find a place to sit. Most of the time, it was by himself. He had a feeling this wouldn't be much different.

Settling on a burrito and side salad, he picked up his food then scanned the massive tent. Only when he was looking around did he see rafters. This wasn't a tent at all but a hastily thrown together building covered with canvas wrapping to appear like a tent. Something potentially long-term that wanted to appear short-term.

As he inhaled deeply and walked to an empty bench, someone waved to him. Millard was sitting by himself as well. He looked so happy to see him, Mark couldn't possibly have said no. He sat down across from him.

"Nice, huh?" Millard said.

"It actually is. When Steven said 'camp,' I was expecting tents in mud."

"That's not the way they do things. VN's one of the top ten companies in the world that no one's heard of. A major Indian corporation. The really big corporations, the powerful ones, no one really knows who they are. But they might know their subsidiaries. I read once that eighty percent of companies that make more than a hundred million a year are owned by only seven corporations."

Mark took a bite of the burrito. The meat was tender and juicy. "That is a damn good burrito."

"Everything's good here, told you."

"Lemme ask you something, Craig, do you have any idea why the hell I'm here? I feel like I'm spinning my wheels, and Steven couldn't be happier."

He shrugged and took another bite of his bloody pink steak. "Who knows? Some jobs here that one man can do have five people doing them. I think they're covering their asses. Maybe they can say you're their liaison to the native population or something."

They ate in silence a moment before Mark noticed something on the man's neck. "What is that? On your neck."

"This?" he said, lifting the symbol on his necklace. "It's Nehebkau. He's the two-headed snake god they worshipped in ancient Egypt. They thought he guarded the entrance to the underworld. The name literally means the 'harnesser of souls.' So it has something to do with my profession, but honestly I just think it's cool."

"You're really into your field, aren't you?"

"Snakes? Oh, yeah. I love them. They're the most worshipped animals in history. And the most mysterious. We don't know as much about them as we like to think. You could have two people standing around talking and have a venomous snake, like a king cobra or a rattler, come by. They could completely ignore the closest person, slither right past them, and bite the other one. We don't know why. The secret's in their tongues, we think, but we just don't know a lot about the tongue. There have been some suggestions in the literature that snakes can actually pick up on diseases, like cancer and HIV, just from licking the air around a sufferer. But again, it's all conjecture. We just don't know as much about them as we'd like. Like why they lost their limbs in the first place. It doesn't make any sense."

He took another bite of steak and chewed thoroughly before continuing. "Even in our own mythology, they're mysteries. In Genesis, the snake tricks Eve into eating the fruit of the Tree of the Knowledge of Good and Evil, but nowhere in Genesis does it actually say Satan was the snake. That's inferred from some things in the Book of Revelations, which was written centuries later. So in our founding myths we have the snake responsible for our fall and temptation, not Satan. Every culture has the same types of myth. The snake as something entirely unknowable."

"Mark, I was wondering where you went." Riki sat down next to him with a cola. She was wearing a hat with the VN logo emblazoned on the front and tilted up just slightly, revealing the features of her angular face.

"The doctor was just telling me about the mythology of snakes."

She cringed. "Well, maybe I can convince you guys to talk about something else."

"It's not all bad," Millard said with a mouthful of meat. "All our medical symbols are associated with snakes, too. From the time of the staff of Hermes and Asclepius from ancient Greece. We've seen snakes having healing properties in the labs, too. Some of the venom was once used to treat broken bones, and the bones actually healed faster with the venom than in the control group. Pretty impressive stuff."

Mark noticed Riki squirming, so he changed the subject. "So how long have you worked for VN?"

"Oh, about a month," Millard said. "I'm actually a professor at the University of Texas. They thought this would be right up my alley, and they were right. I can't tell you how much my colleagues would shit their pants if they knew what I was doing here."

"You didn't tell anybody?" Riki asked.

He shook his head, his fork scraping the last bit of meat off the steak and separating it from the pale fat. "Couldn't. But, and this is why I'm here, I get one. A small one, a baby if we can get it. Can you imagine? I'll have an allegedly extinct species in my laboratory and get to raise it from infancy."

Mark was about to ask what good that would do but stopped himself. He had known several professors in his time with the LAPD—they taught seminars on a host of subjects to police officers—and their sole motivation seemed to be publishing as much as they could. It led not only to tenured faculty positions but also to the much more coveted corporate consulting gigs. He had no doubt Millard thought this little endeavor was going to land him some serious cash and recognition.

Riki said, "So you've devoted your life to studying these animals, and you're okay just killing them?"

He shook his head but in a manner that said she just didn't understand. "Snakes, the species as a whole, will never go extinct. If this were lions or mountain gorillas, then yes, I would have a serious problem with it. But snakes are nature's survivors. They were here four hundred million years before us, and they will be here hundreds of millions of years after. They reproduce at incredible rates. In Florida, about five hundred Burmese pythons got out of a shipping warehouse because of Hurricane Andrew. A few years later, we had a population of ten thousand Burmese pythons in the swamps of Florida. They were even eating alligators. They're perfectly adaptable. They can grow until the day they die, dependent on food supply and temperature. Because they're cold blooded, the warmer the temperatures, the bigger in size they'll get. And if it's cold, they'll stay small. Like the *vipera berus*, which can be found in the Arctic Circle. They'll live even if this company kills tens of thousands of them."

After eating half his burrito, Mark pushed the plate away. "Steven seems to think these particular snakes are the biggest in the world."

"They are. I haven't seen one yet, but I've talked to several of the workers that have. And if it's true... oh, man. I just can't even tell you how excited I am if it's true." He wiped his hands then his lips with a napkin and threw it on his plate. "See you guys later. I've got some preparations to make."

"Sure," Mark said.

"Odd little man," Riki said when he had walked away. "Loves his snakes."

Riki glanced around. "I was in the administration tent after you guys had left."

"Oh, yeah?"

"They've got two computers there. I looked at one of them, over the shoulder of the guy who was on it. Apparently it's on some secure server and has a permanent chat and video window open for some VP of the company."

He shrugged. "That's not unusual."

"You don't think it's unusual to have a VP on permanent chat? What could he possibly need constant updates about?"

"Money that's being spent, probably. Who cares?"

"No, I don't think so. That can be done with spreadsheets and email. Something's going on here that we're not being told."

"We're not being told anything, so that wouldn't surprise me. I just want my money, to work for a month or so, and be done. I don't need to know anything about what's going on."

"You don't care if it affects this island?"

"Of course I do, but there's nothing I can do about it. Leave that to the politicians."

"I talked to one of the workers. Told him it was for the piece I was writing. I tried asking him about everything that was going on with the company, but he wouldn't talk about that. All he wanted to talk about was the snakes."

"What'd he say about 'em?"

"He said they're not snakes. He thinks they're de-

mons sent by God to punish us."
        "Who knows? He may be right."

25

The first patrols would be going out tonight at 9 p.m., and their shift would end at 9 a.m. They would eat all meals out in the jungle and handle all toiletries there. For twelve hours, no one in the teams would return to camp for anything.

At around seven, the sun began a slow descent back into the earth. For the first time since he'd come here, Mark actually felt anxious. It was one thing to sit in a tent and try to think of things to say, another to hunt for large animals in the jungle.

In his time in Peru, back when he thought he was going to live there, he'd seen plenty of anacondas and boas. One had even snatched a small child from the village in which he was staying. The snakes, some of the local villagers had told him, were like snipers. They picked a place to set up then didn't move until prey approached. This particular anaconda had set up right outside the doorway of a home. When the boy stepped out to go to school, the snake struck. Some of the other children came by a little later and saw the snake eating the boy. The villagers killed the snake, but it was too late. The village felt it was an omen, and they blamed all the foreigners, including Mark.

He bounced around from village to city for a year or so then decided he wanted something more tropical with less crime. He had been mugged twice and his flat broken into more times than he could count. No alarm systems existed in the rural villages, and the villagers protected their own over the foreigners. So, he had come to Fiji. He'd seen a really nice photo posted on Twitter once and on a whim hopped on a plane.

So while not exactly a world traveler or snake expert, he'd seen enough of them to know what they were like. Anacondas were relatively easy to kill if found. He'd even seen a villager in Peru kill one with his bare hands by lifting the snake at the back of the head and snapping its spine. Mark kept telling himself he had nothing to fear, but something about the jungle at night unnerved him.

He followed Steven to the open clearing where the twelve teams had gathered. Each was receiving instructions and their packs, checking their GPS, back-up maps, and flashlights. Mark waited around until Steven told him which team he would be on.

"You and me, brother," Steven said with a wide smile.

The team consisted of Mark, Steven, and two native islanders named Qasim and Kapoor. There were enough people that neither Steven nor Mark should have had to go out, but Steven insisted it was part of his contract.

"It's hard enough getting the lazy-ass islanders to work," he said. "I'm not giving you up unless I have to. Besides, you don't need to do nothing. Just point and shoot if you have to and only if you have to. I'll do the actual killing; you just tell me if you see one of them bastards."

Before the teams headed into the jungle, Riki ambled up to Mark. "Be careful," she said.

"I will."

"I got something for you," she said. She handed him a little charm made of a smooth stone. "There's a guy in a tent selling them. It's a tortoise. It's supposed to ward off snakes."

"Well, not exactly what we're trying to do, but I appreciate it just the same." He slipped it into his pocket. The teams were heading off into the thicket of trees and vines. "How about we grab a drink when I get back?"

"Anytime."

He grinned and turned to join his team.

They were on a relatively clear path, the same one used to come into camp, the only way in or out. They trudged single file for a good quarter of a mile before they broke off in different directions on different trails.

Mark followed Steven, and the two natives hung back behind them. He didn't speak—none of them did—for a good long time, but Steven was whistling some song Mark didn't recognize.

"You like Rascal Flatts?" Steven said from up ahead.

"Never heard them."

Steven looked back. "Don't they get music on the island?"

"We're about five years behind the States, if the stuff makes it over at all." Mark looked around. The sun was nearly set, and darkness was enveloping them. "Where we headed?"

"Each team is going in a different direction. We've cut out paths everywhere, so we're just gonna find our path and head up."

"That simple, huh?"

"Well, we'll change tacs soon enough. We start with the low-hanging fruit. Any of them snakes on the sides of the trails, we take 'em out. Then we'll work our way farther into the jungle. Kind of like a sweeping circle pattern. We'll hit it all, don't worry."

"About how long you planning on being out here?"

"Long as it takes, I guess. At least until our damn workers stop disappearing."

They hit a hill, and Mark pumped his legs as his thighs burned from the incline. "You keep saying disappearing, but they're not disappearing, are they? They're getting killed."

Steven glanced back at him, his face a dim outline in the darkness. "Whatever you want to call it."

Within minutes, Mark couldn't see anymore without his flashlight. Steven had put on his goggles, but he didn't want to do that just yet. He would use as much light as he could. Something about the goggles struck him as silly. Maybe the fact they had to use such advanced equipment just to find some snakes.

The carved-out trail wasn't neat or clean. Men using machetes and probably axes had cut it through the jungle, just enough of a trail so they could follow it and not have to cut a new way, but certainly not easy. Several times, some sticky or sharp plant caught Mark's arm, hand, or leg, and he'd have to tug it away.

As they went farther into the jungle, the moon rose in the sky and the canopy thinned. The light was enough that Steven turned off his goggles and got out his flashlight. But the thicker jungle canopy farther in blocked the moonlight, and he put on his goggles again. This time, Mark did the same. The flashlight just wasn't illuminating enough surface area for him to quit running into things.

The night vision goggles gave everything a bright

green glow. The people around him were brighter than the trees and the ground, and he figured that objects giving off more heat were also giving off more light, or something like that. It occupied his mind to come up for reasons for it, and he thought about it a long time as they disappeared into the heart of the jungle.

Mark looked behind him. Qasim and Kapoor, their heads down, machetes in their hands to cut away any loose branches. Mark wondered why he didn't get a machete.

Once complete darkness had fallen, with the canopy overhead hiding the moon, the jungle was about as dark a place as Mark had ever seen. He occasionally lifted the night-vision goggles and was just amazed at the blackness.

Steven pulled something out of his pocket. It resembled a harmonica, but he pressed a button on it and it gave off a low, rumbling-type sound.

"What's that?"

"Something the Professor made for us. Based on some Native American tribe that used a wind instrument to attract snakes."

"Does it work?"

"We'll know soon enough."

The device changed pitch every once in a while, but it only went lower. Then when it hit the bottom note, it began to climb again. The sound didn't seem completely out of place here, and it soon faded into the background below Mark's conscious awareness.

The bush thinned out enough that the men behind Mark stopped using their machetes. He could see ahead about fifty yards, and there was nothing but vines, bushes, and trees. They arched around in a circle, and

Mark thought maybe the trails were cut as constricting circles with the camp at the center. That would likely be the most efficient way to secure the area around the camp.

Suddenly, Steven held up his fist, indicating to stop. Mark froze in his tracks as the two men behind him did the same. Steven scanned the jungle around them. He turned the volume up on the little device he was holding.

Mark saw nothing. The jungle seemed to move on its own, as it always had.

Steven's gaze stopped just off to their right, facing a thicket of trees. Mark intently watched the area as well. He tried it with the night vision goggles then shone his flashlight over the area with the goggles still on but saw nothing. He turned the flashlight off.

"How big did you say these snakes are supposed to be?" Mark whispered.

"I don't know. Big enough to take down a man, that's for sure."

They waited at least two or three minutes before Steven relaxed and said, "Okay, let's keep moving."

Mark's senses were more aware as the men trekked through the jungle again. Fear, or at least anxiety, had now taken hold, and he had to recognize it. Though he had never really been afraid of the jungle, other than the insects, since he'd moved here, he understood why many of the locals had told him the jungle was a sinister place where demons lived.

They looped around the camp for several hours until Steven said it was time to stop and hydrate. They ate jerky and drank water out of canteens. Qasim and Kapoor didn't speak. Mark asked them a few questions, but they just gave one-word answers and kept their eyes away, a signal in their culture that they didn't wish to speak to the person talking to them.

Steven was busy on a GPS then his satellite phone, which was getting little service. The voices that came through broke off frequently, and static obscured them.

"We're going to be at this for twelve hours?" Mark said.

"Just nine more to go, brother."

"Steven, I can't walk for twelve hours a day. That's too much. Especially in the dark."

"Who said anything about walking? We do three on foot and then post. Every team has a place they're posted, and this is ours. We'll be here the rest of the night."

"And the snakes are just supposed to come to us?"

"With a little help." Steven motioned to Qasim.

Qasim reaching into the pack lying next to him. He opened the inside pocket and pulled out a trash bag about a third full. Laying the trash bag on the ground, he pulled out the carcass of what looked like a rat the size of a French bulldog.

"What the hell is that?" Mark said.

"Capybara," Steven said as he walked over and lifted the rodent. "Anaconda's favorite meal. Imported fresh from South America."

Steven took some rope and metal hooks out of his pack. He thrust the hooks through the flesh of the rodent then attached them to one end of the rope. He flung the rope over a branch and tied down the other end, leaving the rodent hanging from the tree upside down. He took out a large hunting knife strapped to his hip and slit the already dead animal's throat. Slowly, blood trickled down onto the jungle floor.

Steven settled back down next to his rifle and said, "Well, I guess we just wait now."

26

The camp was buzzing with activity as some of the field workers were returning. Riki hadn't actually seen any of the oil fields out here, and she wished someone would take her out. The idea of oil fields on an island was counter-intuitive, though possible. It must be, otherwise they wouldn't spend all this money.

She walked through the camp and received many stares from the workers. As far as she had seen, she was the only female in the entire camp. She thought maybe in the administrative branch there'd be some, but there weren't. No managers, no secretaries, no IT, no women. The only conclusion she could draw was that they had purposely excluded women.

The electric lamps illuminated every row of tents, but they only went so far. Past a certain point was just darkness, though not empty. She felt eyes on her. She decided it wasn't a good idea to walk around without protection and made up her mind to ask Steven for a pistol when he got back to camp.

The one thought that kept coming to her, though, more than the need for a weapon, was whether Mark was all right. He had kind eyes, no deception in them. And the way he did his best to hide his attraction to her was adorable. The men in Los Angeles were forward and blunt. Relationships for her age group, mid- to late twenties, seemed built around love of alcohol and partying rather than love and respect for the other person. She made up her mind long ago that she would rather be alone than in a relationship based on that, but the prospect of living in paradise with Mark gave her butterflies. Considering they hadn't even gone on one date yet, it became idle conjecture. She'd been on plenty of dates with men she thought she would get along with, only to find something deeply flawed about them.

She hurried to the administration tent, sticking close to the center of the path and away from the tent entrances. The plethora of languages spoken by the men she passed was astounding. She considered herself a polyglot but couldn't even identify some of the regional dialects.

The administration tent was a building, not a tent. She'd seen that the first time they brought her here. It indicated VN intended to be in the jungle for quite some time. She stepped inside, glancing around once to make sure no one was watching her. How odd that they would leave this place without anyone to guard it, she thought. From a plastic board on one wall, sets of keys hung on hooks. Probably to equipment and cases with sensitive materials inside.

The two computers in the back were on, and she cautiously stepped over to them. She scanned for cameras but didn't see any. The chair creaked as she sat and queued up the computer. She didn't recognize the brand, and was trying to find a logo when she realized it was a VN computer, probably custom made.

The server was connected, and she quickly scanned the names of the people to whom the computer was linked. She took out her phone and opened a note-taking app. She began typing in the names. A couple names were familiar as bigwigs with VN, but some weren't familiar at all. And one name completely surprised her: Thad Nelson. One of the United States senators from Alaska.

"Excuse me," a male voice said behind her.

She spun around, knowing she had shown too much surprise, though she tried to cover it with a wide smile.

"Hi," she said shyly.

"Who the hell are you?"

"I'm Riki Howard, with the *L.A. Times*. I was hired to document this expedition."

"What expedition?" The man stood rigidly with his hands behind his back and his chest puffed up. A military man if ever there was one.

"The one to kill the snakes."

The man didn't speak for a moment. "Oh. Well, you can't be in here."

"Sorry. Steven said I could kind of wander around."

"Anywhere but here."

She nodded and stood up, slipping her phone back into her pocket while she grinned at the man. "Sorry, was just seeing if I could check my email on here."

Riki brushed past him and glanced over her shoulder once while at the entrance to the tent. He was still staring at her, and she smiled again and walked out, her heart pounding. Outside, she turned in an arbitrary direction, acting as though she knew where she was going, and took out her phone. She looked at the names again. Background searches would have to be done on each, but the senator was the most fascinating. *Why would a senator need constant access to an oil company drilling for oil on some remote island?*

As she looped around to her own tent, she decided she had to find out. But before she could enter her tent, she saw a group of four men about three tents away. They were all facing her as they smoked. They neither smiled nor said hello, just stared.

Riki thought she might not wait for Steven and see if she could find a gun right away.

27

Mark took off his boots and socks to let his feet air out a bit. Walking for three hours didn't seem like it would be that exhausting, but he felt like he'd just run a marathon. And the humidity and heat was unrelenting. In the deserts of California, where he and his ex had spent some time camping, the temperatures at night dropped to forty or fifty degrees and rose back up in the midday to over a hundred. In this jungle, that wasn't the case. Apparently, the heat never let up.

He looked back to the giant rat, or whatever the hell Steven had said it was, hanging from the tree. All the blood had seeped out through the slice in its throat, but nothing other than a jaguar or leopard had come by for a look. They heard its growl, and Steven lifted his rifle, scanning around the rodent. "Can't have someone steal our snake snack, now can we?"

Mark would've stopped him. The big cats were endangered and protected on the island. And aside from that, they were damned beautiful. He wouldn't let one end up as some ornament on Steven's wall.

Mark checked the clock on his phone: 5:34 a.m. He stretched his back, put his socks and boots on again, and stood up to get some blood in his legs. Their shift ended at nine, so that left three and a half hours. He could do three and a half hours.

"You all right?" Steven said, lying on his pack.

"Fine."

"Not a jungle person, are you?"

"How could you tell?'

"'Cause you got this, like, scrunched-up look to your face all the time. Like you're smelling something bad."

Mark placed both hands on his lower back and pushed, arching his back to stretch it. "Why am I here, Steven? Really. No company bullshit. You don't need me."

"Oh, on the contrary, I do need you. More than you know."

"Then why don't—"

"Shh."

This time, Mark heard it, too. A slight crunching of foliage, as though something heavy were traveling through the bush then stopping as soon as it made noise. They both turned their heads in the direction it came from. Mark wished they had a fire, but Steven said it would drive snakes away. At least, Millard had told him that was possible. Though again, he said the science on snake likes and dislikes wasn't a hundred percent certain.

Qasim and Kapoor had been dozing, but they were fully awake and alert now. One of them pulled down his rifle and slowly rose to his feet. The other one's eyes were wide, as though he were listening with them instead of his ears.

"Qasim," Steven whispered, "you and Kapoor flank it. Me and Mark are gonna come up from behind."

Qasim nodded and disappeared. Steven slid on his goggles, and Mark did the same. The jungle lit up around him, and he let his eyes adjust before moving. He picked up his rifle and followed Steven, who was working his way through the brush.

They pushed their way through the thick shrubbery, making far more noise than Mark would've liked, then circled around behind the clearing they'd been sitting on. Steven was in a high crouch, but Mark just walked. He hadn't exactly done this before and didn't quite know how to act. The last thing he wanted was to crouch, trip on a vine, and accidentally shoot his team leader. He had a feeling he wouldn't get his paycheck then.

They stopped momentarily and listened. Mark thought they were listening to Qasim and Kapoor, but something else suddenly popped out to him: the jungle was quiet. All the hoots of the monkeys, the squall of the birds, the cheeps of the insects, all silenced. A cold feeling, like ice water poured down his spine, flowed down Mark's back.

Steven held up his hand and motioned with two fingers to keep moving. Mark crouched lower.

The canopy was thin overhead, and with the goggles on, the glare from the moon was nearly blinding. The goggles worked by enhancing the little light there was, but the moonlight here, without any light pollution, was as bright as a light bulb. Mark wouldn't be taking the goggles off, though. He just squinted as best as he could and tried not to look directly up at the sky.

Soon, they were near the hanging rodent. Steven flipped off the safety on his rifle, and Mark followed suit. He swallowed. His mouth was dry, and the only thing he could hear was his pulse pounding in his ears. They were nearly behind the rodent now.

Just as Steven parted the brush to step behind the rodent, a scream echoed through the air then loud pops of gunfire. Steven jumped out of the brush. Mark froze. Only through sheer force of will, he lunged forward with his rifle held out in front of him.

Qasim was firing at something in the bush. Steven joined him; Mark lifted the rifle and pulled the trigger. The kickback was something he wasn't expecting, and the rifle nearly flew out of his hands. He stabilized it and continued to fire. The rounds were tearing through trees and brush, vines splintering off and flopping to the ground. Mark didn't know what he was firing at, but he didn't stop. Not until Steven had stopped first and shouted at Qasim to cease firing.

Qasim was breathing heavily, his eyes wide as golf balls.

"What was it, what'd you see?" Steven said.

"I don't know. It's in there," he said in his accented English.

Steven held the rifle in front of him and cautiously walked toward the brush they'd been firing into. He moved the vegetation aside with the barrel of the rifle and looked in. Steven stepped to the side and spread apart the brush. The body of a big cat—a leopard, Mark guessed—lay on its side. He stepped closer. Clutching the rodent between its jaws, the cat was motionless, not breathing. So many bullet holes filled it that Mark could see its internal organs.

"Well, hot damn," Steven bellowed. "Good shootin', Qasim."

Qasim didn't change expression, still sucking in breath as if he'd taken a run around a track. Mark lowered his rifle then slung it over his shoulder. He looked around.

"Where's Kapoor?"

Qasim's smile faded. He looked around as well. Steven's face lost its smile, and he scanned the surrounding jungle.

The cold feeling on Mark's spine was back.

They had split up and searched for over an hour. There was no sign of Kapoor until Steven found his pack. The pack had been lying on the trail not far from where they had hung the rodent. Blood spattered the back. They searched until the sun was up. Mark's feet and back ached. The pack was weighing him down, and he felt every ounce of its weight against him.

The three men met up near a small clearing. Steven tilted up the hat he was wearing and wiped his brow with the back of his hand. He looked around the surrounding jungle. "He's gone."

"Qasim, what did you see?" Mark said.

The man shook his head. "I saw the leopard. I started shooting. Kapoor was behind me."

"You didn't see anything else?"

He shook his head again, staring blankly at the ground with a devastated expression on his face.

"Kapoor was his cousin," Steven said.

"I'm sorry," Mark said. "If he's out here, we'll find him."

"No, he is not here. He is dead."

No one spoke a moment then Steven said, "Let's cut out early tonight."

Mark had expected Steven to be distraught at another disappearance, but he seemed downright shaken up. Maybe because it was so close to home. That could've been any one of them. As they hiked back to camp, none of them spoke.

Once in Tent City, Mark didn't ask what to do next or where to go. He just walked to his tent, dropped his pack, kicked off his boots, and collapsed onto the cot. Workers coming and going and the day hunting party trading shifts with the night caused commotion outside, but Mark's exhaustion was so deep he didn't care about any of it. He closed his eyes and drifted off to a dreamless sleep.

28

Groggy and weak, Mark awoke sometime around midday. Sweat had soaked his shirt right through to the cot. He swung his legs over and sat still a moment, orienting himself. Then last night came to him. He ambled out of the tent, squinting from the bright sun overhead. The camp was busy, but no one seemed to pay him much attention. He went to the latrines then to the mess hall. His stomach growled, as he hadn't eaten in somewhere around fifteen hours.

The mess hall was always open, it seemed, but if someone missed the designated times, they apparently had to eat leftovers. Mark found some soggy sandwiches bloated with mayonnaise and grabbed a ham and cheddar with a bag of chips. He grabbed bottled water from an icebox, chugged it completely, and got another one before sitting down by himself.

He ate in silence, watching the other workers coming and going. Some were jovial, but most were despondent. Looking like they were digging their own graves, he thought. And suddenly, he didn't want to be here anymore. No amount of money was worth disappearing because of whatever the hell made Kapoor disappear.

It wasn't just snakes. Quicksand, venomous spiders,

leopards, poisonous plants, any number of things that filled the jungles could've killed Kapoor. Whatever it was, it wasn't Mark's problem. This was a waste. He would inform Steven today that he was leaving.

"Hey."

Riki was coming toward him. She grinned and sat down across from him. Despite the heat, she still looked lovely, her cheeks flushed red and her hair held up in a bun.

"Thought I'd find you here," she said. "How was it?"

"One of our men disappeared not ten feet from us."

"Disappeared? What do you mean?"

"I mean disappeared. We found his pack and it had blood on it. He was gone. I'm guessing he didn't hightail it back here, either."

She swallowed. "Was it..."

"I don't know what the hell it was." He looked around. "I'm getting outta here, Riki. This isn't worth it. We need to leave, both of us. We don't belong here."

She shook her head. "I can't do that."

"Why not?"

"Something's going on here, Mark. Something deeper than searching for oil and disappearing workers." She leaned close. "Remember those open IMs I found? There's one linked to a senator from Alaska. Why would they possibly need that?"

He sipped his water. "I don't care. This is, whatever the hell this all is, it's bigger than us."

"That's exactly what I'm saying. These people are doing something huge and I'm guessing illegal. I want to find out what. This is my job; I can't just leave."

"Even if it means risking your life?"

"I don't feel I'm doing that. I'm not going into the jungle, and I don't have any plans to."

He shook his head. Despite his desire to leave, somehow he couldn't leave her here. Not here. Not to Steven. He would be staying, too.

"One day," he said. "You've got one day to find whatever you're looking for. And then I'm pulling you out of here. And if you fight me, I'll tell Steven what you're up to."

"You wouldn't... okay. Okay, that's fair. One day."

29

Mark hadn't seen Steven all day. A rumor had been going around the camp that he'd killed one of the snakes and was in the jungle using it as bait for more snakes, but somehow Mark knew that wasn't true. Something else was going on.

Mark strolled around camp with Riki. She talked to whatever workers would speak to her. Most didn't have much to say, but a few did. Some told them they'd heard the hunting parties had all been killed; some said they'd killed all the snakes and it was safe to go back. Mark was curious how the other teams had actually performed and tried to track Steven down.

The administration tent was now buzzing with activity. Steven slumped in a chair. Yesterday, he appeared nearly invincible, a man completely immersed in his element. Confident in his abilities to get everything done he needed to. But that wasn't how he looked now. He appeared pale and defeated. His shoulders slouched, and he seemed like he could fall asleep at any moment. He was giving commands to some of the assistants but from a sitting position, as though too tired or too lazy to stand.

"Can we talk?" Mark said, poking his head in.

"What do you need?" he said.

"I was just curious how the other hunting parties did."

Steven was quiet a moment. He looked at one of his assistants and barked an order about sending some documents somewhere. "Why are you curious? Don't want to go out again?"

"I'd like to know what my chances are if I do decide to go."

Steven exhaled. "We lost eight men total. One entire team and four from other teams, including ours."

"Eight?" Mark grappled with the number. Eight people dead, just like that. No animal he had ever seen would be capable of devastation like this. "Did anybody see anything?"

"No. One person thought he saw a shadow grab one of his men and pull him into the trees. That's it."

"Well, the hunt's over, right? I mean, we're not going back there."

"Hell yes, we are."

"What? Are you insane? You just lost eight men. One of them right in front of you."

"I was paid to do a job, and I'm gonna do it. You were paid, too. If you want to cut your losses and run, go ahead."

Something in Mark wanted to lash out. To show Steven he wasn't the type of man to back down from a fight. It was almost like a playground dare, one that had to be completed or the cowardice never forgotten. But no way Mark was going out just to get killed. Especially since he was planning to leave tomorrow with Riki.

"You got anything I can do around the camp tonight?"

"Around the camp? Like throwing away trash or something?"

Mark blushed. "Never mind."

He turned to leave, and Steven said, "I think there's some maid outfits at the supply tent."

Mark ignored the comment and kept walking. Unsure whether his anger was directed at Steven or himself, the number eight kept going through his mind. Eight men dead in a flash. *What the hell was out there?*

Mark spent most of the day sleeping, eating, or walking with Riki. He'd found out she was a French major in college, along with journalism, and they spoke briefly in French. Mark's father had been French, and he'd actually lived in Bordeaux for a few years as a child. The little French he remembered was exactly something a child would recall. Nothing substantive, just terms related to play, food, and basic conversation.

At dusk, Mark was sitting in his tent on the cot, debating what to do. Riki stated she could only get into the administrative tent late at night when no one was there, so they were definitely here one more night.

The thought of going out into the jungle again filled him with dread. Not that he was cowardly, but just that it was so futile. Last night, a man was taken right in front of them. They'd been outsmarted and outmaneuvered. Only a fool went up against greater forces knowing he was going to lose.

Millard, the herpetologist, poked his head into his tent. "Hi," he said, upbeat.

"Hi," Mark said. "Something you need, Craig?"

"I'm, well, I'm going out with your team tonight, and I was wondering if—"

"Are you crazy? Do you know how many people disappeared last night?"

"Well, no, but I thought that—"

"We don't even know what's causing it. But whatever it is, it's smart. It outsmarted Steven, anyway. You're not coming."

"Well, no offense, but I don't work for you. I just came to ask if you knew where an extra pack was? We don't seem to have any more."

Mark scoffed. "There's one with blood on it out in the jungle. Help yourself." He rose and brushed past the man. He made a beeline for the administration tent and found Steven sucking on a cigar outside of the tent. "You can't let Millard go," Mark said. "He's inexperienced."

"So are you. You did just fine."

"It's different. He's going to get himself killed."

Steven shrugged. "He's a big boy. Let him decide for himself."

Mark stepped close to the man. "What the hell is really going on?"

Steven blew out a puff of smoke then looked to the horizon. The sun was nearly set, just a shimmering orb quickly disappearing behind pink clouds. "Come tonight, and you and I will talk. I'll tell you everything."

"No games? No company talk?"

"No games. I'll tell you exactly what's going on here."

"Okay, I'll come."

As he walked back to his tent to pick up his pack, the last of the sun's rays lit the sky before darkness fell.

30

The pack seemed heavier than it had last night, but it was actually lighter. Mark took out anything superfluous and kept the essentials. He didn't know whether he'd hike back through the jungle at night by himself, but the plan so far was to learn what was really going on then get the hell out of there. Assuming Riki obtained everything she needed.

He slung the pack over his shoulders and trudged through camp. It was quieter than usual. No one was playing games, and though the men drank, they drank in silence.

Riki was waiting for him near the gathering teams. Though only eight had disappeared, at least two-thirds of the men from last night were absent. Steven was yelling at some men in a different language.

"What's going on?" Mark asked.

"Apparently the men are refusing to go back. They're demanding triple the pay," she said.

Mark watched the argument for a moment then said, "I'll be heading back myself tonight. And we're leaving. We'll try and take a Jeep if we can, but if not, we're walking."

"Walking through the jungle at night by ourselves?"

"I'll take my chances in the jungle over these people any day. Just be ready."

After a few minutes, the men reached some sort of resolution. About half left, and half stayed. Steven waited until all the other teams left before walking up to Mark. "Just the three of us," he said.

Millard strained under the weight of a pack. He was already sucking breath and was wearing shorts.

"You can't seriously be taking him out," Mark said.

"He's a set of hands, that's all we need." With that, Steven began tramping up the path into the jungle.

Mark looked back to Riki. She had a look of concern on her face and said, "Hurry back."

"I will."

Night fell so quickly Mark had to fumble in his pack to find the night-vision goggles. He hadn't anticipated having to use them this early. He flipped them on and saw two bright figures in front of him.

Millard was breathing heavily now and constantly sipping out of his canteen. His boots were high-end, but the laces were undone on one of them, and he walked in them as if he was unaccustomed to them. As though new and never worn before.

"One of your laces is undone," Mark said.

"I know. I keep it that way. For luck."

"How is that lucky?"

Millard shrugged. "Just something I've done since I was a kid. Don't really remember how it started."

Soon, the jungle completely enveloped them, and only a slit of moon was out tonight. Gray-black clouds covered it, and only the faintest glow of white was visible on the edges.

The heat was even more unbearable than the previous night. It came from everywhere; the sky, the trees, the ground, surrounding Mark on all sides and pressing in on him. Sweat made his shirt cling to his back, and it rolled down his forehead. He had to stop several times and drink from his canteen. Only after about an hour did he realize he didn't have enough water to last the entire night.

One hour turned into two. By the end of that second hour, Millard was struggling. Even in the green tint of the goggles, Mark could see that sweat soaked him. Each man carried three canteens, and he'd already gone through all three, foolishly dumping some water out on his head to cool off a few times.

"You okay?" Mark asked, himself breathing hard.

"I didn't expect it to be this hot."

"Here." Mark handed him one of his canteens. "Don't dump it out on your head. Just sip it slowly and only when you have to."

They looped around the same path they had on the previous night, but at a fork in the trail, they took another route. Mark didn't say anything, thinking Steven knew what he was doing and they'd all end up in the same place again eventually.

Another twenty minutes passed, and Mark was obsessively checking the time on his phone. Service was almost non-existent.

"Right here," Steven said. "It's as good as any place." Steven unloaded his pack but kept his rifle slung over his shoulder and his goggles on. Mark dropped the pack as Millard did the same. Millard found a fallen tree to sit on, and he groaned as he stripped off his boots and stretched his legs.

"Mark, I think I saw something over there," Steven said. "We better check it out. Let Craig rest."

"Okay." He figured it was just an excuse to talk. He followed Steven about thirty yards farther up the path. They came to a small precipice, maybe fifty feet from the jungle floor. Below them the trees and shrubs were so thick he couldn't see what lay beyond.

"I will say this, brother, this is the damned prettiest jungle I ever been in."

Mark's legs felt weak and sore. He sat, placing his rifle down next to him. Steven took a few paces around before coming to rest beside him. He gazed down at him and took off the goggles as Mark did the same. The dim sky was beginning to shine as the clouds moved on, and the stars sparkled like gems, providing just enough light that they didn't need the goggles anymore.

"So what is it?" Mark said. "What're you guys really doing here?"

Steven slipped the rifle off his shoulder and removed the safety lock. He was glaring at Mark, unblinkingly, a frozen expression on his face. "Well, see," he said quietly, "about that. They're doing some interesting stuff here on your little island. And I just can't have reporters and ex-cops looking into everything, now can I?"

Mark's heart raced, and he began to reach for the weapon next to him. Steven lifted his rifle, pointing it at Mark's face.

"That's a damn shame that Kapoor died last night," Steven said. "It was supposed to be you."

Mark swallowed. He had to buy time any way he could. "That's why you brought me out here? To die?"

Steven chuckled. "You think I'd bring you on a hunt with me? Some washed up cop hiding in a shack? No, brother, you were not my first choice."

"What's going to happen to Riki?"

He shrugged. "Ain't no women around. Maybe I give her to the workers as part of their incentive package to keep hunting with me."

"You can't beat whatever's out here. You know that."

Mark desperately scanned the area around them. If he reached for the rifle, Steven would fire. He didn't have enough time to get to his feet and run. That left one option, but even that would take a second or two, and Steven could get off some rounds.

Footsteps behind them, and Millard appeared. "What the heck you guys doing?"

Steven looked over. As he did so, Mark jumped.

He leapt from the precipice, slamming into the side of the canyon and sliding down on his butt. Debris and pebbles flew up into his face. He snagged on something sharp, and it spun him. He went head over heels, smashing his head into a tree stump before he rolled to his side and stopped only when he hit level ground.

His head was cut and bleeding. Above him, he heard shouting and shots fired before Mark closed his eyes, unable to stand.

31

Something was different about the camp. Riki could feel it. The men were more subdued, whispering in quiet corners. Everyone was on edge, and when Riki went to the mess hall for something light for dinner, it was empty. No one was working, and no food was out.

She returned to her tent to wait to sneak into the administrative tent again late at night. This time, she would snap photos and forward emails to record what was going on. Maybe she could even find some files they didn't want her to find.

As she entered the tent, she noticed those men again, the ones standing a few tents away and glaring at her. The same four from the previous night. This time they said something in another language. The man that said it grabbed himself, and the other three men grinned like vultures. She stepped inside the tent and zipped up the flap. Her gaze never left it as she backed away. There was no doubt in her mind now; no one was here to help her. Not the company, not Steven, and even Mark was gone. She was alone. And these men didn't care about laws or the police, because no one even knew they were here.

That left two choices. She could sit here and hope nothing happened, or she could try to find that gun she wanted.

With every bit of courage, she opened the flap of the tent and stepped outside. The men were still there, and now they appeared curious—not curious enough to follow her, she hoped. She turned quickly away from them, and when she heard a conversation in English, she immediately stepped into the group and said, "Hi, you guys Americans?"

They spoke, the mundane chitchat of people too exhausted to do anything else. She answered when she was supposed to and asked questions when appropriate, but her attention was on the four men near her tent. They were smoking and eyeing her as if no one else was even there.

After a few minutes, she slipped away from the group and continued through the camp. A few tents held supplies for the men. They received a certain number of vouchers to spend at those supply tents, buying candy bars, chips, and other snacks. Riki hadn't been to one of the tents, and she wondered if they had weapons, too.

She was about to ask someone where the supply tents were when she noticed a man walking toward her, or in her general direction anyway. The man from last night, the one that had caught her in the administration tent. Two other men flanked him. When they saw her, they quickened their pace.

Riki instinctively knew to get away. She took a few paces back then turned and hurriedly walked in the other direction. Glancing over her shoulder, she saw the man rushing to catch up to her. Whatever they needed, she could tell from their faces she wanted no part of it.

As she passed her tent, unsure exactly where she would go, she felt a hand on her arm. One of the four men, which she had completely forgotten about in her panic to get away from the others following behind her, had grabbed her.

"Where you going?" he said in a thick Eastern European accent.

"Let go of me."

"Maybe you come to our tent," he said with a sly smile. "We have beer."

"I said let go."

"Let her go," someone said behind her. It was the man from last night.

The worker looked at the man and lost his smile. He didn't let go of her arm for a moment then slipped his hand away. Neither of the men said anything to each other, and the man behind her turned his attention to Riki.

"You'll need to come with me, Ms. Howard."

"For what?"

"Because you're under arrest. Now come with me, please."

"Under arrest for what? What is this about?"

"Ma'am, if you don't come with me, I am authorized to use force to bring you in." He stepped to the side, motioning with his arm for her to walk in front of him. "Please, come with us."

Riki weighed her options. Nothing sounded appealing, but going with the men who at least had some semblance of civilization left was the safest choice. She stepped through them and strolled casually through camp as though nothing were wrong, the men circling her as they headed wherever they were taking her.

32

Mark hadn't passed out, but he wished he had. The pain was so intense he rolled to his side just in time to spew out whatever he'd consumed that day. He couldn't remember exactly what he had eaten, and it worried him. He raised his hand to his forehead. It didn't come away with blood. The blood had dried. He had been lying there for a while. The events of the past few hours returned to him, and he remembered Steven and his rifle.

He had no weapons, no night-vision goggles, and nothing to eat. He had to get moving before his energy left him or Steven found him.

Mark tried to force himself up but nearly collapsed from the pain. Everything hurt, from his toes to his head. He rolled to the side and lifted himself up on both elbows. Then his palms, then his knees. He let out a groan so loud he felt like a ninety-year-old man. Though the pain was ever-present, he could get into a kneeling position, which meant nothing major was broken.

A quick evaluation of the pain told him he had at least torn something in his right shoulder and possibly fractured a rib. But his legs were largely all right. When he felt he wouldn't do further damage, he rose to his feet with a grunt of pain.

As he was about to turn, he heard a noise behind him.

He had no energy left to fight. He was hollow and empty, and if Steven was there, he had won because Mark could do nothing to fight him off. Slowly, Mark turned his head. A figure strolled up to him. There was nowhere else to run.

The figure was wearing shorts.

"You all right?" Millard said.

"I thought you were dead."

"Bastard shot at me, but I took off. What the hell is going on?"

Mark grimaced from a throbbing fire that shot up his leg into his lower back. His sciatic nerve. "I think you and I have been duped, Professor."

Millard placed Mark's arm over his neck and helped him stumble through the jungle. After a few minutes, when the blood had returned to his legs, Mark walked on his own. The pain had gone from intense burning to a powerful soreness. Mark couldn't tell which hurt worse.

Neither of them had any gear to cut through the thick shrubbery. Most of the vegetation tugged at Mark's clothing and skin, leaving scrapes and bloody punctures.

As they pushed through a thicket of trees, they came to a small path. Almost like the trail they had walked with Steven but narrower. Meant to be walked single file.

"They'll be on the trails," Mark said.

"I don't know about you, but I can't fight through a jungle all night."

Mark thought a moment then nodded. "Okay. Just keep your eyes open."

Their pace wasn't much faster than the lazy stroll of a cat. Inch by grueling inch, Mark fought to keep stride with Millard, who frequently stopped to let him catch up. The heat was less intense now, but it was a wet heat that sucked all the moisture out and left Mark like a bag of dry sand.

The clouds had moved on, fully exposing the moon. The light was enough for them to get by on the trail but nothing else. Mark wouldn't have been able to navigate anywhere except a ready-made path.

"Your phone working?" Mark asked.

"No service. Yours?"

"Lemme check... No."

"If we can make it back to camp, they'll—"

"We're not going back to camp, Craig."

"Why not?"

"Steven wasn't acting alone. This was planned. This is what VN wanted. Or at least implicitly consented to. Steven wanted me dead, and now you're a witness to it. There's no way they're letting us out of that camp alive."

Millard thought a moment. "Shit. Shit!" he shouted. "Fuck me. I did not sign up for this!"

The statement was so ridiculous Mark would've chuckled if it hadn't hurt so much. "We don't need camp. We can make it out on our own. The cities and villages are all on the shores. We just have to keep walking in one direction, and we'll eventually hit a beach."

Millard nodded, his hands on his hips as he looked up to the moon. "Do you know I haven't even got tenure yet? That was my goal for like ten years, and I'm gonna die without doing it."

"Well, let's just keep walking, all right?"

"Yeah, all right," he said, like a child accepting a chore they didn't want to do.

As they walked, Mark's pain increased but not in a debilitating way. The important thing was to keep moving, and his legs did just that. A dull, radiating pain throbbed from his thighs and lower back though, and he worried he had injured his spine.

The trail led deeper into the jungle, not away from it and to the shore. Right now, they had no other options, nowhere else to hike.

Mark kept up as best he could, but occasionally Millard pulled so far ahead, lost in thought, that Mark wasn't able to see him anymore. A small panic gnawed at him. Not that Millard could do anything to protect Mark, but just the thought of someone else there, someone else's presence, was enough to comfort him in this hell, and he marveled that he even cared. He hadn't known that about himself, how much he really needed other people.

They walked for what Mark guessed was a couple of hours. The jungle grew denser and hotter. Finally, Mark couldn't move his legs anymore. He had to drag each step out of himself until he stopped.

"I can't go anymore," he said, out of breath.

Millard turned. He was exhausted as well, as evidenced by the deep, nearly frantic breaths he was drawing. "This is as good a place as any to rest, I guess."

Mark collapsed. He sat down so fast the impact against the ground hurt his tailbone. He leaned back on his arms, but that hurt too much so he slouched forward. The thought of lying directly on his back on the jungle floor didn't sound appealing.

Millard sat down next to him, and they were quiet for a moment, listening to the jungle sounds. The monkeys were loud in this area, and for some reason that comforted Mark. He remembered the silence of the other night, the deathly silence that preceded one of their men disappearing without a trace.

"Are snakes smart?" Mark said.

Millard shook his head, staring at the ground. "No. One of the smallest brains for body size in the animal kingdom. Why?"

"A man disappeared from my team last night."

"Yeah, I heard about that."

"If it was a snake last night that took that man, it sure as hell acted like it was smart. He distracted us and then struck when our attention was on something else."

"Impossible. That's higher brain function. They just don't have it. Snakes are opportunists. They lie in wait, hit a target, and if they get it they get it. If they don't, they move on to another target. They can't reason the way you're suggesting. I think this particular genus would have to be smarter to survive as long as it did undetected, but not that smart."

Mark focused on drawing in as much breath as he could. The mugginess made it harder to breathe, as though he were sucking air through a straw. "You really believe what's out here is a prehistoric snake?"

"I do. The coelacanth is a sixty-million-year-old fish. We thought it was extinct, until we found out that some fishermen in South Africa had been catching them for decades. And this is a big fish, up to six feet long, and we had no idea it existed. There are still plenty of things in the world we don't know about."

"But why here?"

"This is the perfect environment for them. They want cover, which they have in the jungle, abundant prey, which again they have, and heat. The hotter the better. They've got all that here. And the fact is we don't know why they went extinct. There was no cataclysmic event like with the dinosaurs. There's no reason they shouldn't still be alive."

"How big you think they can get?"

Millard stretched his legs out in front of him. He sighed and looked up to the sky before answering. "It depends. They'll grow until they die, so theoretically, they can get huge. I've seen anacondas over thirty feet. An explorer I admire, Percy Faucett, said he saw one over sixty feet when he was exploring the Amazon basin. He wasn't the type of guy to exaggerate, so I would take his account as truth."

After that, they didn't speak again for a long time. Mark slumped over and closed his eyes. He was worried that sleep would overtake him so fast he would just topple over, but the opposite was true. Sleep never came. Every inch of him screamed for sleep, but his mind wouldn't allow it. As if it knew the dangers and had decided it wouldn't follow Mark's conscious direction anymore.

"Should we get moving again?" Millard said.

Mark nodded and slowly climbed to his feet.

33

Riki noticed two guards near the entrance and one around back of the administration tent. As the men escorted her there, she ran through different scenarios in her mind. They could offer her money to keep quiet, which would be the ideal. Or they might want to kill her. It was also possible they intended to do something in between. Maybe send her away, have her fired, sued, something like that. She just didn't know, and the men that brought her to the administration tent weren't speaking.

The man from last night gently nudged her inside. He told the others to wait outside. He stepped into the tent with her and said, "Have a seat."

Riki did as he asked. She sat down, her back straight, and tried to appear as confident as possible, though inside she was a mess. If they knew how afraid she really was, they would use it against her.

"Tell us what you were doing in the tent last night?" the man said, sauntering to a table and pouring a glass of water out of a clear jug.

"I was just trying to check my email. I don't have phone service out here."

"Bullshit." The man sipped his water. "You're not gonna like how I get information that I need, Ms. Howard.

And I need that information. I need to know what you were doing in this tent."

The man was calm and collected, speaking smoothly and without apprehension. She imagined he had done this a thousand times and knew what she was going to say before she said it. *So*, Riki thought, *what would throw a man like that off?*

The only thing she could think of was the truth. It might buy her some time until Steven and Mark got back. Maybe even allow her to get back to her tent, at which point she would slip away in the middle of the night. Mark had been right. Better to take chances with the animals in the jungle.

"I was looking for information about what your company is doing on the island. I'm a reporter for the *Los Angeles Times*. My bosses know I am here, by the way, and with your company."

The man looked surprised for a moment. Just a flash that came into his eyes then quickly faded away. "Reporter, huh? Well, what exactly do you think is going on that is so important you came out into the middle of this jungle for?"

"I don't know. Why don't you tell me? Your company hired me."

He smirked and finished his water. "See, here's the thing, Ms. Howard, there are no police here. There's nothing here but my men. Men we pay that are loyal to us. So I think you should probably just answer my questions and save the attitude for the mainland." He paced around her, settling on a desk against the wall. He leaned against it and stared at her before speaking. "What exactly did you find out?"

She shook her head. "Nothing yet."

"You're lying."

"No, really. I know you have some instant messages set up to various executives, and that's it. I was going to try to find out more tonight."

"Give me your phone." She handed it to him, and he flipped through it before slipping it into his pocket. "I'll be hanging on to this for a while." As he walked out of the tent he said, "You may want to get comfortable. Might be a while before we decide what to do with you."

34

The trudging had turned to the most grueling exercise Mark had ever done. Before this, he had always thought he could walk forever. It didn't strain anything and was pleasurable. Now, each step caused his muscles to light on fire. He pushed for as long as he could then needed to rest. Millard stayed with him, though Mark got the impression he was happy to rest as well. Every inch of jungle looked the same as the last, and neither one knew where they were going. If they had been walking in circles, Mark wouldn't have been able to tell.

As the sun rose, it painted the clouds pink. The sky was a layered texture of blue and pink, stunningly beautiful. Mark wished he could focus on it instead of his situation. They were lost in a jungle with no food or water, and he was injured. The chances of making it out were remote, to say the least.

He was grateful for the trail. Without a path already cut out of the dense shrubbery, he would've collapsed a long time ago.

"Can you go any farther?" Millard asked.

Mark nodded. Millard had to help him up each time, and he did so now. The man, despite Mark's impression of a sheepish professor, was kind and calm under pressure.

Not at all like the first impression he had given.

They hobbled along the path, slowly but with few stops. Mark watched the sky as much as he could. He'd lived on the island for over four years, and he'd never seen the sky like this. Not that the sky was different from any other morning. The difference was his appreciation that he had lived to see another day.

"What's that?" Millard said.

Mark looked forward, a slight jolt of anxiety gripping his guts. But no one else was around. Millard was looking at the jungle floor up ahead of them. He hurried over and bent down. It was a pack, one of VN's.

A single thought hit Mark, and suddenly nothing else was important. "Check for canteens."

Millard opened the pack and ruffled through. "Jackpot!" He threw one canteen to Mark and kept another for himself. Mark tried to restrain himself, only taking a few gulps, but it was as though he were fighting his own biology. His body screamed for water and didn't stop screaming until the warm liquid doused his tongue and slid down his throat.

He drank a third of the canteen. Millard had drunk nearly all of his. Millard flipped through the pack again and found the MRE. He ripped it open. Mark sat down next to him, and they ate the powdery, dry food. It was chicken enchilada. Mark had once heard a serviceman he knew call MREs "three lies for the price of one: they weren't meals, they weren't ready, and you couldn't eat them." But no meal had ever tasted quite so good.

They scarfed down the meal and finished it with some water. As they were lying back, enjoying the sense of food in their stomachs, they heard a wet crunch, loud and echoing, from slightly behind and off to the side.

Millard rose to his feet.

At first, Mark could see nothing but jungle. Then something came into focus between two large trees not twenty feet away from them, like one of those paintings where one sees something if they stare at it long enough.

He noticed the scales first.

Black and slick, they looked like obsidian. Shimmering in the light, quaking with each contraction of the enormous muscles underneath.

Mark's breath quickened, and his heart beat in his ears. As his gaze followed the colossal body, he came to loops. The snake had coiled itself around something.

The *something* was a man.

The coils were like massive pipes, each much thicker than the width of the man. The man was completely horizontal and exposed only from the chest up, the rest of his body wrapped in the snake's blackness. The man was still alive. He was blinking, blood pouring out of his eyes and nose.

The coils tightened. It was little more than a shudder, but the force crushed the man to pulp. The pressure exploded his skull, causing brains and blood to eject over the jungle floor.

Then Mark saw it.

The head was about three feet wide, with black eyes the size of melons. The snake moved gracefully through the air as its tongue flicked several times. In a flash, it closed around the man's lifeless corpse.

It began to swallow the corpse whole.

Millard was breathing so heavily, Mark was scared the snake could hear it. Millard shook his head several times then finally stammered, "It didn't even need to unhinge its jaw."

Mark slowly stepped away, but Millard was frozen. He either couldn't or wouldn't move. Mark had to grab his shoulder and physically pulled him away. Once Millard was moving up the trail, Mark picked up the pack, slung it on his shoulders, and followed.

The pain in his body suddenly didn't bother him, and his pace was quick. He kept up and even overtook Millard. When they were far enough away, the men looked at each other but didn't say anything for a long time. Not until they had walked for so long that what they had seen seemed like a distant memory.

"I never..." Millard mumbled. "I mean, I knew they'd be large, but I mean, that thing couldn't fit through a doorway. I had no idea." The fear in his voice faded, and excitement replaced it. "I mean, what does a creature that size eat? What's its natural food source? Even the biggest rodents would just be snacks. I bet it eats crocodiles and giant turtles. I mean, a thing like that could eat anything it wants."

"There are no crocodiles in Fiji."

"Then it's gotta go somewhere where there's larger prey. The ocean, maybe. Can you imagine an animal that size in the ocean! Think what it could eat! It would be the top predator in these waters. And what about—"

"Craig," he said, cutting him off, "my only concern right now is that we're on that thing's menu. So let's just focus on getting the hell outta here."

They managed to walk maybe a hundred feet before Millard began again. "It's been undetected all this time. One of the biggest animals on the planet, and it's been hiding in the middle of an island. I wonder if you were right? If maybe it's evolved over the past fifty-eight million years and has something resembling basic reasoning.

Intelligence. I mean, how else could something like that remain hidden from us?"

Mark ignored him and kept walking. The shock of what he had seen hadn't worn off. He had no words, no explanations, other than man wasn't meant to see something like that. Because every time he blinked, the image was there. Like it had burned itself on the insides of his eyeballs.

After a good hour, the weight of the pack finally got to him and the adrenaline had worn off. The pain returned, and Mark found every step a struggle. But he'd be damned if he was going to stop and rest here.

He dropped the pack and began throwing things out. No weapons were inside, and most of the supplies were unnecessary for getting through the jungle as fast as possible. He kept the water, the food, and the night-vision goggles. He strapped the goggles to his wrist and tucked a canteen in the front of his trousers and an MRE in the back. Millard did the same, and they left the pack on the trail as they started again.

"We have no idea how long snakes can live," Millard said. "Can you imagine how old something like that might be? With no natural predators, it could be hundreds of years old."

Mark stopped and turned to him, looking him in the eyes. "Craig, I don't want to hear about that thing anymore. All I want to hear is if you have any idea how the hell to get us out of this jungle. If you don't, then keep it to yourself."

Millard looked hurt, and Mark instantly felt bad. Millard had been kind to him, and he didn't deserve that.

"Look, I'm sorry. This is all just too much for me. I'm not handling it well."

"It's okay. I'm sorry, too. I get excited about it. I've devoted my life to studying snakes, and the granddaddy of them all just appeared in front of us. It's like a paleontologist finding a live T-Rex or something."

"I know, and I'm sure you'll have plenty of time to study them later. But for now, let's just focus on staying alive."

35

By midmorning, the heat had returned. Not that it ever really left, but with the addition of the sun, the jungle became a boiling caldron. They drained the water in the canteens fairly quickly, and Millard asked if there were any rivers with clean water nearby.

"I don't know," Mark said. "I've never been in this far."

The more they walked, and the more they sweat, the more exhausted they became. Mark's muscles tightened up, and each movement grew more difficult because of the dehydration. His lips were dry and would soon crack and bleed, releasing even more of his precious moisture. He could take these conditions a couple of days, maybe even one more than that, but if they were lost for too long, the snakes would be the least of their concerns.

The snakes.

As soon as Mark thought that word, it sent a small shiver up his spine. He had momentarily, in the pain and fatigue of forced exertion, forgotten about what he had seen. With that single word, it came back to him. The man's pale flesh as his brains spattered out as though being shot from a small cannon, the blood that splashed on the snake's slick black flesh, the fangs like butcher knives, and the enormous murky gullet of which Mark only caught a glimpse when it opened its mouth and took the man in.

The scene was so gruesome, so outside the bounds of anything Mark had ever expected to see, he would never be the same. Something had happened that changed the way he saw the world and his place in it. He wondered if people with post-traumatic stress disorder felt that way.

"What's that smell?" Millard said.

"I don't know."

Mark had picked up the scent a long time ago. Like a tangy exhaust in the air. Almost citric.

Millard stopped by the side of the trail, his gaze on the trees. Mark glanced over and at first didn't see anything out of place then noticed what Millard was glaring at. The trees appeared pale. The leaves were a light green in splotches, white in others, as though losing their color. The bark was falling off in small pieces, like chipping paint.

"Are you looking at the trees?" Mark said.

"These flora are all sick. They're dying."

"From what?"

"I don't know."

They stood in front of the trees a while, and the more Mark watched them, the more he understood what Millard meant. The trees' pallor, in any living creature, meant only one thing: impending death.

"Let's keep going," Mark said.

"I'm not sure we should go in this direction. The smell's coming from this way."

The only other option was to turn around. That meant backtracking almost two days and passing that... *thing* again. "We've got no choice. I'm not turning around."

Millard breathed for a bit before answering. "Yeah,

me neither."

The trail widened as they progressed, and the undergrowth thinned. The trees appeared paler the farther they went, until many were just withered, dying husks.

As they approached an open clearing, the smell in the air became nearly unbearable. Mark had never smelled anything like it before, but it had a familiarity to it. Like the black exhaust that had hung over Los Angeles in the '80s.

As they approached the clearing, they came across a rocky hill, what could've been a small mountain with a flat top. Around the base crews of workers operated heavy machinery. And just off from the base, workers occupied a large pit. About six inches of dirty water filled the bottom, and the workers had formed a line, sifting through the water and passing things back along the line. They loaded whatever it was they had found onto the backs of utility trucks.

"Gold," Millard whispered.

Mark ducked low to avoid being seen. Millard remained standing, wiping the sweat from his brow, and Mark grabbed him and pulled him down. "A gold mine?" Mark said. "In the middle of the jungle?"

"Some of the best gold mines in the world are in jungles. Look at that, though." He pointed to the outskirts of the mine. "All the vegetation is dead."

Mark followed the perimeter of the mine with his eyes. All the trees, the shrubs, vines, bushes, flowers, and grass were dead. Nothing but brown matter covering bare dirt.

"That's from cyanide," Millard whispered. "It's called gold cyanidation. It's the most efficient technique for extracting gold, but it releases cyanide into the air. It gets into the plants and water, the animals eat the plants, and the people eat the animals. Cyanidation is illegal in most countries. I've fought it in the Brazilian rainforests because it was killing off the local amphibian life."

Mark was quiet a moment. "This is what they're hiding. It's not about oil at all. The oil was a distraction."

Millard shook his head. "Clever. They're gonna pull as much gold as they can and in the process kill this entire jungle. I've seen it before. The inhabitants, even on the shores, won't be able to use the jungle for anything. It'll just become mounds of dirt. Even the soil gets poisoned and won't grow anything."

Mark was mumbling, more to himself than Millard. "This is why they couldn't let me or Riki know about—"

Riki.

She was back at camp by herself. Mark couldn't even guess as to how much money VN could make on an illegal gold mine where they paid no taxes or import/export fees. He had already seen to what lengths they would go to protect their interests here.

"We have to get back to camp," Mark said.

"Are you nuts? We gotta get outta here and alert someone about this."

"Who?"

"The UN and then Interpol. I bet there are people in the Fijian government that would flip out if they knew all this gold was being taken and no taxes were being paid."

"I don't care about that right now. Riki's at the camp by herself. If they tried to kill me, they'll try to kill her."

Millard wiped his nose with the back of his finger. "We can't walk back. I don't have it in me."

"These workers aren't walking. There's gotta be some

Jeeps or something nearby." Mark scanned the mine. "But I don't see anything."

"I think the workers were picked up every day."

Mark sat down onto the dirt. "Then we'll wait here for our ride."

36

Other than lack of conversation, the administrative tent wasn't the worst place Riki had been forced to spend time. Once, while on assignment in North Korea—an assignment she'd only taken because she was young and stupid enough to believe her government would actually do anything if she were caught and arrested—the police had detained her.

They figured out she was a reporter when she had been asking a nearly blind man a series of questions. The medical facilities in North Korea were non-existent, a fact that Kim Jong Il had blamed on the West, using propaganda to inform his people the West had blockaded North Korea and was not letting in medical supplies. An accusation whose opposite was actually true. The United States tried desperately to donate medical supplies and medicines, which Kim Jong Il refused.

The nearly blind man had had surgery recently. A British doctor had been allowed into the country to perform several glaucoma and other eye surgeries. At his own expense, of course.

The operation restored the man's vision, and when Riki asked him how he felt about the British doctor who had risked his life and spent his own money to help him, the man replied that he hoped the doctor had been arrested and put on trial for being a Western spy. Then he praised his leader and thanked him for the marvelous gift bestowed upon him.

Riki had never seen that kind of blind devotion, and it frightened her to her core. Everything human about the man, his compassion, his reason and independence, had been taken away from him. He was a slave. A man that had submitted to a slavery machine very willingly and accepted his lot.

Her questions prompted the man's wife to call the police. They arrested Riki and held her in detention for nearly a week. They gave her a room of bare cement walls with bars and nothing else. Not even a toilet or sink. They brought food to her, all stale or rotten of course, and allowed her to use a rank bathroom once every other day. At night, she heard the screams of other women held in the facility as they were raped or beaten.

When they finally released her, due more to the efforts of the *Los Angeles Times* than the United States government, she took a hiatus from her career. She wasn't certain she was willing to endure the horrible things journalists went through for a story. One journalist she knew had been gang raped by nearly two hundred men in Egypt's Tahrir Square. They were shouting that she was a Jew and she deserved it. She only survived because a non-profit group that had been there to attempt to reduce the number of sexual assaults used flame-throwers on her attackers to get them to back down.

Riki did not believe that any story could possibly be worth that risk, and since then, she had gone to free-lance and investigative journalism, rather than covering anything to do with geopolitics or war, the two fields in which most reporters liked to specialize.

Given all that, her circumstances here at the camp were not that bad, and she was at least grateful for that. Though whether she was going to survive or not still hadn't been determined.

By evening, she was thoroughly bored. They'd brought her food once, but other than the two guards stationed inside the tent with her, they left her alone.

"Could I at least get a deck of cards to play solitaire or something?"

The men glanced to each other but didn't respond, and she realized they didn't speak English. Riki sighed and sat down in a chair, leaning her head back. At least Mark and Steven would be back in a few hours, and that would—

"Hello, Riki."

Steven stepped inside the tent. Dirt covered him, with stains on his neck and face. He set down on a desk the rifle he was holding before he took off his canvas vest and slung it over a chair. He sat down as he exhaled loudly and closed his eyes.

"Boy I tell ya, if you're on your feet all day, nothing feels quite as good as just sitting your ass down in a chair for a minute."

"Where's Mark?"

"Well, here's the thing, Mark got some crazy ideas in his head. I don't know what exactly, something about us being an evil corporation and violating laws or something. Damn fool just ran off into the jungle."

Riki swallowed. "Is he dead, Steven?"

"I just told you he ran off into the jungle. You got shit in your ears or something?"

"Where in the jungle? Is he alive?"

"I doubt it. You see, these snakes, they're getting

more active. Have been the past few weeks. Think it might have something to do with the blasts we're doing in the center of the island. The damn snakes have been coming closer and closer to camp. We even had a few people taken right outta their tents, though I hid that up pretty well. So I don't think lover boy's chances of surviving out there without any weapons are very good."

She shook her head. "Why? Why are you doing this?"

He slipped out a pack of cigarettes from his pocket. He lit one, inhaled, and let the smoke billow out of his nose. "Because I'm paid to protect certain people and certain things. Protection doesn't just involve physical protection; it involves protecting information, too. Information that you want to take."

"I don't want anything from you. I just want to go home."

He exhaled another puff. "See, now that's where we have a problem. I know you know something, but the only way to ensure you tell me is to get it out of you."

"What're you talking about? I don't know anything. I told what's-his-name last night everything I knew."

He took out a hunting knife from his boot and placed it on the desk before leaning back in the seat. "Lemme finish this cigarette, and I guess we'll find out."

37

Evening fell quickly over the jungle. Mark and Millard hadn't really spoken. Small talk about jobs or where they'd grown up seemed ridiculous, so they remained quiet and watched the workers.

The labor was backbreaking. Mark couldn't imagine working like that day in and day out. The men seemed to take it stoically, barely stopping even to take a drink of water. Mark watched them until he grew bored, then he closed his eyes and lay back in the dirt. He stared at the sky as it changed from blue, to gray, to black. When night had nearly fallen, he heard a whistle and the work stopped.

Mark got to his feet. Millard was snoring loudly, and Mark lightly kicked at him. "Let's go. Quitting time."

They trudged down a hill, careful to go down the farthest side to avoid being seen. Once they were near the pit, they simply melded in with the crowd and followed them out to a loading zone where large trucks allowed them to climb into the beds. Mark climbed into one and helped Millard up. They sat on the side in silence, neither one with the strength left even to speak. Mark felt like he was dying a slow death from exhaustion and knew he could've fallen asleep right there. It took everything he had to fight that urge.

Mark hadn't seen the road they traversed. It was smooth, not paved over but almost like the dirt had been flattened to allow for easier travel. The road led straight through the jungle but never narrowed and was never bumpy. It had taken some time and effort to clear out this path.

As the jungle canopy enveloped them, Mark simply couldn't fight anymore. He was about to ask Millard to help him stay awake, but the professor's mouth was open, and he was snoring again.

Mark closed his eyes and was gone.

38

Steven finished his cigarette in silence, and Riki realized it was packed with marijuana. The pungent smoke filled the tent, giving everything a gray haze. She knew the smell well from college, but she had forgotten about it. A scent buried deep in her mind somewhere that brought up memories of running to classes she was always late for and awkward fumblings with boys in her dorm room.

When he finished the cigarette, he put it out then stood up and stretched from side to side. He picked up the knife and let it dangle in his fingers. He had changed. He'd seemed friendly before, almost kind. Now his eyes held something completely different. Something akin to a hungry animal staring at food.

"You don't need to do this," Riki said. "I've already told you everything."

He nodded but still took a step forward.

"Steven, stop. Stop it, you're scaring me."

He grinned, his eyes bloodshot and glassy. He stood over her, the knife at his side. The blade reflected the lights in the tent and glimmered brightly. Riki couldn't take her eyes off it. No matter how much she tried to look up at the red-rimmed eyes, to reason with them, to buy herself more time, she couldn't do it. Her gaze refused to move from the knife.

"Steven..."

"You know, I killed only one woman before. In the Sudan, back there 'bout five years ago. She was giving us a helluva time, 'cause we'd killed her husband. She even slapped me. Right there in front of my men." He chuckled. "Ten of us standing there armed to the teeth, and she thought she could get away with it. Anyway, I shot her in the face. Point blank, closer than you are to me now. I saw that light go out of her eyes and her body crumpled, kinda like puppets do when the puppeteer leaves. I tell you, girl, killin' a woman is a lot different than killin' a man. No matter what they tell you." He held up the blade. "But you're the first I'm gonna be real up close and personal with."

He took a step forward, and Riki's heart dropped into her stomach.

Before he could make a move, a scream tore through the air. It was coming from outside. Steven turned around, staring out the flap of the tent. He hesitated a moment then walked over.

In a flash, Riki was on her feet. She grabbed the rifle he'd laid down on the desk and swung it at him like a baseball bat. The butt of the rifle slammed into the back of his head. He flew forward, collapsing against the entrance flap. Half his body lay outside and half in. She hadn't knocked him unconscious, but he was disoriented. Riki jumped over him. He reached up, his right hand catching her calf. She kicked him in the face. His grip loosened, and she pulled away then ran.

The camp was in chaos, men running with no method to what they were doing. No dash for an exit. Everyone was just sprinting, and it didn't seem to matter which direction.

She raced past the tents so quickly she fell. She caught herself, and gravel stung as it cut into her palms. As she stood up, she wiped her palms on her pants and ran again. Some of the tents looked familiar, and she realized she was running by her own tent. She didn't know what was happening. The chaos was such that no one would've told her anyway. Panic had taken hold, like a herd of cattle in a stampede.

Riki ran into her tent and zipped up the flap. She backed away from the entrance and nearly stumbled onto her back. She stood quietly and listened to the cacophony of shouting, screaming, and gunshots. Her hands were trembling so badly she gripped one with the other and tried to steady them.

A tearing sound filled her tent. The zipper on the flap was opening, and someone stepped through. One of the men that had stood near her tent and stared at her. Behind him were two of the others. They zipped up the tent behind them.

Riki backed away. She turned to run somewhere, anywhere, but there was nowhere to go. Two of the men grabbed her and forced her to the ground. She kicked and scratched, but they pinned her arms down while the other held her legs. The man that had stepped in first stared down at her, a smile exposing yellowed teeth. He slowly unfastened his belt and released his zipper.

The flaps to the tents opened with hardly a whisper. The men focused completely on Riki, but she spotted the movement and turned her attention toward the flaps.

The serpent's head was massive, the width of a couch. Its tongue whipped out of its mouth silently only once before it discovered what it was looking for. Its body followed through the entrance and seemed to never end. Black with red speckles, it shimmered in the light of the tent's single lamp.

The man pulled down his pants just as the serpent slithered across the floor like water, wavy and flowing quietly. The head, close to the floor, shifted beneath the man then spun around as though made of clay. The mouth opened, and it jolted forward like lightning. Fangs sank into the man's stomach and genitals. The man's face contorted into an expression of pure pain and terror. He tried to pull away and screamed as blood spewed from the corners of the snake's mouth. The more he struggled, the more flesh tore away from him.

The snake lifted him up and flipped over, the man upside down, the fangs embedded between his legs. He screamed such a guttural, desperate cry that Riki wanted to cover her ears.

The serpent's full body slid into the tent, filling the entire space. The tail end wrapped around the man's chest and head, muffling his screams at first then stopping them completely as a series of loud crunches emanated from within the writhing mess of flesh.

The body flopped on the ground, and the man's head turned completely around, staring up blankly at the roof of the tent while his stomach lay against the ground. The serpent coiled around and opened its prodigious mouth. The lower portion took in the man's head, and it slowly worked down the body.

The two men holding her down froze in place. They had all watched the bloody carnage unfold in front of them and hadn't moved. It seemed to take place in slow motion, but really the entire incident lasted no more than a few seconds. The serpent killed with such efficiency, its movements appeared smooth and planned, as though the entire kill had been foreordained and the serpent merely executed nature's will.

The men jumped up and sprinted out of the ten, leaving Riki on the ground by herself. She crawled backward, as far from the snake as she could get. When she felt the back of the tent, she slowly got to her knees then her feet. At a snail's pace, she eased out of the tent, past the gargantuan animal in front of her.

The sounds it was making as it swallowed the body were something out of nightmares. Wet, hissing, sucking noise. Some sort of slime covered the body as it entered the throat, and the snake's eyes were staring forward, ignoring her completely. She sneaked past it.

Down the path to the administration tent, she saw one of the men that had held her down. A snake had torn his head off with a single bite and was swallowing the headless corpse. But another man ran by, and for some reason, he diverted the snake's attention. It regurgitated the corpse and slithered after the man that had run past it with a speed that shocked Riki. The snake moved as though it were swimming, an effortless wave over the ground that curved its body into an S.

The coils wrapped around the man and lifted him into the air, crushing him to a pulpy mess. The snake would have no trouble swallowing him, as he was now little more than a liquefied sack of meat. Riki sprinted away. She was numb, her mind a blurry mess of sensations and impressions but no thoughts, as if her reasoning mind had shut off and the only thing left was a blubbering mess of instinct.

She ran in a sea of darkness speckled with only the occasional lamp light. It reminded her of running through neighborhoods as a kid. She'd run through darkened streets, and then streetlights would light everything up for about twenty feet before fading to darkness again. Direction wasn't something she possessed right now, no sense of which way she was going. Occasionally she passed crowds of men, and at other times, she was by herself, running past empty tents like a city of ghosts.

She rounded a corner and saw with horror that the Jeeps usually lined up as transportation for anyone who needed it were gone. The last one's taillights were just barely visible as it sped up the road then disappeared.

The wind was blowing, and she stared at the spot where the Jeep had been, her hair whipping her face. A heavy feeling started at her head and worked its way down into her chest and guts, past her hips and into her legs. The feeling was resignation, a deep resignation that told her she was going to die here.

But she decided she wasn't just going to lie down and let it take her. She scanned the area around her, found the closest path into the jungle, and dashed toward it, disappearing into the trees without looking back.

39

The trucks arrived, and Mark only woke because someone shook him. He opened his eyes and roused Millard. The men were walking into camp. Mark climbed out of the truck and stood for a moment, orienting himself. He felt groggy and weak, the pain from his injuries beginning to throb again. The first stop back in civilization would have to be the hospital.

Millard stumbled out and onto his back. He groaned, still half asleep. Mark helped him to his feet, and they followed the rest of the men back into the thicket of tents. But something was different.

No conversations, no music, nothing. The wind through the tents, shaking the electric lamps, debris fluttering on the ground... but no people.

The rest of the men, roughly fifty of them, were debating what to do. Mark didn't understand what the problem was until he happened to look into one of the tents. Something on the floor appeared at first like a ball, or perhaps crumpled-up clothing, but with streaks of red on the side. He took a step closer. A human head, severed from the body with the ragged flesh of the neck hanging off the bottom.

Mark backed away slowly. He didn't have the

strength to react properly. Didn't have the inclination to spend any energy thinking about what it meant or what could've happened. He just wanted to get Riki and get out of there as quickly as possible.

The men were talking loudly, and the volume was increasing. It continued for a few moments before the argument turned to shouting and then, seemingly out of nowhere, men began to run. Mark heard a sound he would never forget, a hiss so loud and long it vibrated his bones, as if the earth itself were blowing air through some great cavern.

The snake slithered between the tents expertly, shooting one way then another, rounding the posts as though it were an obstacle course it'd gone through a hundred times. It was much faster than the men, much faster than any man Mark had ever seen. A blur of movement rocketing through the camp as though it required no effort to move.

Mark couldn't take his eyes off it as it slithered into a crowd of men, and they screamed one horrible shriek in unison as they realized someone was going to die.

As that snake targeted its prey, another came from the opposite side. It wrapped itself around one of the men so quickly, his legs were still kicking as the serpent raised him into the air. The man screamed only for a moment before the coils wrapped around him, and no part of him was visible anymore.

"They're attacking in unison," Millard mumbled. "They're working together. Snakes don't do that."

"What the hell are they?"

"I don't know."

Another hiss from another direction, and another, and another. The snakes were pouring in from all sides.

Mark and Millard hadn't gone far enough in to be part of the trap, and they both instinctively backed away. The two men broke into a run back to the truck.

Seven trucks had carried all the men back, and all seven were there, but no drivers. Mark checked the first truck for keys but didn't find any. He ran from one to the next, but none of them had keys. The drivers had taken the keys with them.

The screams were at fever pitch now. Mark looked back and saw an ocean of slithering flesh. Blackness was surging into the group of men. The snakes left them only one route of escape, and the men took it. But as they did so, more of the animals seized them from dark corners. A trap perfectly laid and executed.

"Come on," Mark shouted. At first, Mark wasn't sure where they were going to run, but there were only two places: up the road to try walking back to the city, or hiding in the jungle. The road seemed too exposed, at least for now. They would be out in the open and, having seen how quickly those serpents moved, he had no doubt one could be on them in a few seconds.

They dashed for the thicket of trees.

Mark couldn't tell how long he ran. Everything hurt, and the pain dulled his reasoning and memory. All he could focus on was the pain. The acid in his legs burnt as though they had been skinned and had rubbing alcohol poured over them. His lungs felt as though they were about to explode, and his mind was a numb, blank canvas of fear and confusion.

The shrubbery scraped his skin, but he barely felt it. It was like the sensation of being anesthetized then having the doctor tug on his flesh. He knew something was happening but couldn't exactly say what.

Millard was doing better. Fear had given him strength, and he was running far ahead, so far that Mark couldn't see him anymore. Just heard his boots crunching the dead foliage and his body sliding past the shrubs and bushes.

The darkness was enveloping, welcoming. He wanted to crawl into as dark a place as he could find and not move. To lie there for days on end and just be left to himself. Away from the jungle and Steven and the whole damned world.

A realization came to him then, though he hadn't put it into words. Not until he came to a small clearing did his conscious mind realize what his unconscious had picked up a while ago. He couldn't hear Millard anymore.

"Craig!" he shouted.

No response. Nothing but the wind of a storm still off shore. The wind was making the trees shake as though they were reaching for him. They swayed toward him then relaxed before their long, gnarled arms reached for him again.

Mark snapped his head to the right as he heard a scream. A pleading, horrible scream. A man's voice, begging and infantile. The voice of someone in the clutches of something greater than himself, shown something he wasn't meant to see.

Sprinting toward the voice, Mark shouted, "Craig!"

Through the trees and a rough patch of bamboo stalks was another clearing. He didn't know Millard well enough to care for him, but the thought of being out here alone in the dark was unbearable. As he thought it, he felt guilty and ran even harder.

Another scream, cut short.

Mark came upon the small clearing and thought it was empty other than the trees, but one of the great black masses in his peripheral vision was not a tree at all.

The animal was upright, standing about ten feet high, most of its body coiled on the ground beneath it. In its mouth was the body of Craig Millard. The serpent lifted its head with the body in it and opened its mouth, allowing gravity to do the work. The body slid down its massive gorge and disappeared into black. The snake closed its mouth, motionless a moment, as though enjoying its meal, then the head tilted forward and the eyes fixed on Mark. In the dim light of the moon, it could almost be beautiful. Its sheer size made it appear like something not from this planet or time, something that had traveled from somewhere else to make its presence known. But in that beauty was pure horror. The lidless eyes, black and soulless, that held Mark, took him in as though he were nothing more than raw meat. The body that had begun to uncoil in anticipation of a chase, and worst of all, the horrible tongue that whipped out as though taunting him to get away.

Mark didn't wait for it to move first, didn't try to conceal his presence in any way. He simply turned and ran. Fear had completely taken over now, and he became painfully cognizant of the full impact of his predicament. He was lost in the dark with something that lived in it.

The serpent regurgitated Millard's body. Mark glanced over his shoulder just in time to see the wet, lumpy mass flop to the ground as the snake uncoiled completely and shot after him like a torpedo through the sea.

Mark pumped his legs. He dashed between the trees

and the shrubs like an expert but couldn't really see them. He avoided masses of black; other than that, he could do nothing but run. His legs were throbbing with pain, and his lower back sent a radiating heat through his hips. He pushed through the pain and kept pushing his legs. He wouldn't look behind him, but somehow he knew it wasn't far. He could feel it.

The camp was nearly empty. Most of the men were gone, and the few remaining were running around like wild chickens. Mark made it only about thirty or forty feet in before the serpent whipped around and appeared in front of him like some apparition. The snake reared up, reaching over fifteen feet, maybe more. It let out a hiss that sent shivers through Mark, the sound resonating deep in his bones. Some ancestral warning sound buried deep in his DNA.

A truck rumbled to life, and the tires kicked up wads of dirt as it raced for the road back to the city. The snake's head whipped around, catching the lights of the truck, the movement, and the vibrations in the ground. Mark stood perfectly still.

The snake rocketed after the truck.

Mark sprinted back into the jungle, but he had nothing left. No strength, no heart, no will. Only the dim awareness that he was still alive, and had to keep it that way for as long as he could, remained.

He collapsed onto the ground, heaving and panting, knowing that was as far as he was going to get.

40

The sound of carnage was not something Mark had ever thought he'd hear again. He had heard gunshots most of his adult life, even a shootout in the street by two rival gangs, something that sounded like he was in the middle of a war. He'd seen dead bodies in gutters and slumped over their cars' steering wheels. He'd seen young housewives butchered and dumped in the canyons surrounding L.A. as though they were refuse, and he thought he'd gotten away from it all. That this island had been his sanctuary, and all of that would slowly fade into the background then go away.

It hadn't gone away. It was right behind him. The screams of dying men, gunshots, the panicked scatter of men that knew they were going to die. Mark listened to it all but didn't have the strength to do anything about it. Even to save himself.

He rolled to his back, about the only thing his body allowed him to do, and waited for the inevitable.

A blur of memories followed. He remembered the day his daughter was born, the happiest day of his life. He remembered taking her home from the hospital and the smell of her that only parents of newborn babies knew. Her first words, her first steps, none of which Mark actually saw but had to watch later on his wife's phone.

The bad memories came to him, too. The slow, painful separation of him and his wife. Both of them seeing what was coming but unable to avoid it. Mark wished he had been better able to discuss what he was feeling and how they could fix it. But neither of them had the words, and the relationship continued to sink so far that they eventually weren't speaking with each other. And then there was nothing left but the divorce.

Mark remembered his mother, too. Sometimes she cooked, not often but sometimes, and she'd let him help. Put in a pinch of that and a dash of this. Turn the oven on, get the drinks out of the fridge. It had meant nothing to her, just a distraction for her son so he wouldn't plop down in front of the TV, but those few moments alone with her took the place of the deep conversations they had never had. The ones that taught him about love and life, about death and women and joy. They never had those ones, never even came close, but they had their cooking.

He hadn't thought about all the memories stored away in four years. The island life had been so joyful and calm that reminiscing about times past wasn't necessary. He had no need to move on from the pain of the past, because just living here soothed the ache.

"Mark!"

He opened his eyes, unaware that he had even closed them. Stars, planets, and distant galaxies draped the sky. A speckled and shimmering blanket covering the earth. It astounded him for a moment before he felt hands on him. He pulled away, his gut instinct to fight even though he had accepted his death. But the hands were soft and gentle. His gaze drifted up and caught a milk-white face in the gloom. Riki.

"I thought you were..." He didn't want to think about that anymore. Not with her right there.

"You need to get up, Mark. Get up right now."

"I can't. You go. Run as far and as fast as you can. Go."

"No." She slung his arm over her shoulders. "Stand up! You are not going to die here. We are not going to die here, you hear me?"

She didn't have the strength to lift him, but she sure as hell was trying. Her body flexed and strained under his weight. Slowly, he began pushing with his legs, and before he knew what was happening, he was on his feet and moving through the jungle again.

His steps were calm and measured, light. The more he moved, the more his strength and will returned to him. He would live. He would live for his daughter, he would live for this island, and he would live for *her*.

"Stop," Mark said, "Wait."

Riki slowed, and Mark looked her in the eyes. He was no more than a few inches from her face. The urge to kiss her came over him, and he chuckled. Even here, on the brink of death, surrounded by blood and gore, the male urge toward the female was still the strongest thing he felt.

He took a step back. "We'll never make it. Not through this jungle. We have to get one of those trucks."

"How?"

"I don't know. They don't have keys in them."

"I saw keys. A lot of them. In the administration tent. I think the drivers brought the keys there and left them for the next shift."

"You stay here. I'll run back."

"No way. You'll never make it alone. We both go."

Mark didn't have the strength to fight her.

From the edge of the tree line, they could see the entirety of the site. It appeared like some prisoner of war camp. Men were huddled in small groups, slowly taken out by shadows. Far enough away that he could see exactly what was happening, he knew it was no random encounter. The animals weren't coming into contact with humans because people had disrupted their natural environment or even because they were hungry. It was an attack. An orchestrated, planned attack.

"How can they do something like this?" Riki gasped.

"Craig thought they might've evolved intelligence. Part of intelligence is working in groups, having social bonds. These aren't snakes anymore. These are something new."

The administration tent was perhaps three hundred feet away from the tree line. Even if he could sprint all the way there, it would take too long. Any number of the serpents would see him, and they'd be on him in a flash.

Mark scanned the other tents. About a hundred feet away, maybe less, was the supply tent. They kept rifles in the supply tent.

"We can't both make it to the administrative tent," Mark said. "We got one shot. I'm going to divert their attention. When they converge on me, you make a run for the keys. Don't look back, and don't worry about me. You just get those keys and get to the truck. I'll meet you there, but don't wait for me. You get there first, you take off."

"No, there has to be another way."

"There's not. And you're faster than me. It has to be you. The supply tent's right there. If I can hold 'em off and surprise 'em, I might be able to sneak away under the back. "It's the only way, Riki."

She nodded slowly, her gaze on the grass. Melancholy darkened her face, and Mark felt the same way, as if this would be the last time they saw each other, but he refused to show it. He had to portray to her that he was confident about this. That he wasn't just sacrificing himself for her.

"Ready?"

She swallowed. "I guess."

Mark slipped out of the bushes and dashed with everything he had toward the supply tent. The wind was in his face, the hot, wet jungle air swallowing him up as if he'd run inside a steaming cavern. His legs wobbled several times, his knees jerking slightly from nearly giving out, but he didn't stop. He pushed harder. Ignoring the searing pain, clearly from a damaged nerve somewhere in his lower back. Ignoring the pounding in his head that told him he was possibly bleeding internally. Ignoring the icy fear that gripped his guts as if being smashed in a vice.

Fifty feet away now.

Acid rose in his throat. His legs were on fire. A short ache slashed through both sides of his ribs, and he didn't know what it was. He imagined bits of fragmented bones loose inside his body. Cutting at everything soft, releasing cupfuls of blood into his body cavity.

Thirty feet away.

He ran a little farther, his legs slowing in response to the pain in his lungs. Then he shouted, "You fucking slimy bastards, come get me! I'm right here. Hey, hey, I'm right here!"

Nothing happened at first. Then, slowly, some of the

snakes leisurely turned, curious as to what was pounding against the ground. Snakes didn't have ears, but he had heard they sensed things through their jaws. So he kept screaming, coupling it with jumping up and down to vibrate the ground as much as he could.

Unhurriedly, the snakes turned to him and slid toward the supply tent.

Several were coming in from the north, one from the south, and the rest from the east. All were homing in on him as if they had sonar. Converging to a single point.

The supply tent was ten feet away. Mark felt like he was going to pass out. A nearly comical memory hit him just then. Running the mile in fifth grade. He wasn't the fittest child, and the mile had nearly killed him. Anyone who ran over nine minutes was required to try again, and Mark certainly would not be one of those people. So he sprinted as fast as he could, vomited his school lunch, and then had to lie on the grass nearly fifteen minutes to recover.

He had that same sick feeling now. Only this time, he forced himself to keep going.

Jumping through the flaps of the tent, Mark saw a wooden table with papers and clipboards on it. Probably used by the supply clerk to log what people were taking. He leapt over the desk, stumbled to the back of the tent, and grabbed the first rifle he saw. Something that looked like it belonged in a modern war.

The rifle was already loaded. He wondered if they left them that way when he noticed the blood spatter on the barrel. Someone else had already had his idea but hadn't survived to tell him about it.

Mark lifted the rifle just as the first serpent poked his head into the flaps of the tent. He lifted the weapon, aimed quickly, and squeezed the trigger. He fired three rounds. The head was so big he hit on all three, the pop of the rifle fire momentarily deafening him. One round entered the serpent's mouth, and it shrieked like a dying cat and pulled out of the tent.

Mark scoured the back of the tent for any way out. There was none. He'd have to cut his way out. He quickly went through several supply bins until he wrapped his hand around a large hunting knife. Just as he was about to cut a flap of tent away, he saw trembling in the canvas up near the wooden beams. The supply tent was like the administration tent, something set up to be here a long time.

The wooden beams creaked as though bearing the weight of something heavy. Mark's gaze turned upward, and he froze. The thing was climbing higher on the roof, searching for a way in. Another noise overtook it from the opposite side of the roof. They were coming in from the top.

Mark slashed a huge gap in the tent just as the wooden beams crumbled like matchsticks under the weight of the enormous animals. The entire thing collapsed, and something heavy fell on him. It felt like a metal beam falling from a skyscraper, nearly crushing him. If it had just fallen a little higher onto his chest instead of his stomach, he'd be dead.

Then the mass slipped off him.

Mark rolled over and crawled on his stomach. He could see nothing in front of him. He heard a series of loud hisses and shrieks. Wrapped in darkness, he thought that was what hell must sound like.

He continued crawling until he was nearly out from under the canvas. The edge was up about six inches, and he could see outside. Two of the gargantuan serpents lay just next to the collapsed tent. They were surveying the carnage, their tongues darting in and out of their mouths so fast he could barely see them.

One lifted its head and arched low then high. The other looped around it, coiling over the neck. The other one shrieked and nipped at it; it uncoiled and faced the creature. Both let out sounds Mark had never heard and would never forget. Something akin to human screams, but not quite.

The snakes twisted around, slithering over the canvas. Mark continued to crawl, holding the rifle, his only anchor in the chaos. He got free of the canvas and continued to creep off to the side, glancing once over his shoulder. About half a dozen snakes gathered over the collapsed tent, writhing in a curled heap of black flesh and scales.

Mark was on his feet and running to the trucks. From the corner of tents, the trucks were lined up about a hundred feet away. Behind him, one of the snakes shrieked as it shot after him, sliding over the ground as though hovering above it. Mark wasn't going to make it.

He twisted around to fire, but several more of the serpents lunged after him. He couldn't hit them all, but maybe he could take one down with him. Just as he raised the rifle, a truck came roaring around the corner. It hit one of the serpents, and the animal swiveled on the ground, coiling up as a defense and capturing one of the other animals behind it.

Riki drove right past Mark, who jumped onto the truck, his arms over the edge of the bed as he tossed the rifle in. In one final burst of strength, he hauled his legs up and rolled into the bed, collapsing onto his back. Behind him, the serpents had grouped together. They were shooting after the truck like missiles, coming in from every angle. One nearly got into the bed. Mark lifted his rifle and fired several times, hitting the serpent in the body until it pulled back.

The truck rumbled through the camp and to the road leading up to the city. Behind him, the serpents slowed then stopped. They had speed but not endurance. They didn't have the stomach for a long fight. He crumpled backward, his eyes to the stars as the truck raced up the dirt path, kicking up clouds in the dark.

41

The closer they got to the city, the worse Mark felt, as though all the adrenaline was leaving his body and pain took over the vacancy. The bouncing of the truck wasn't helping. He pounded on the back window and motioned for Riki to pull over. Once she had, he crawled out of the bed of the truck and staggered over to the passenger door. He got in and shut the door with a groan. He had never been more aware of his body than he was right now.

"You okay?" she said.

"No, definitely not. If you don't mind, I'd like to stop at the hospital."

She leaned over suddenly and kissed him. It wasn't erotic in any way, nothing sexual, just a small token of her affection. He wished he'd had the strength to kiss back.

She pulled away and drove again. Mark watched the passing jungle before them, dark and foreboding. He wondered what ancient people thought about it, whether it was a place haunted by demons or a source of a beauty and wonder. He didn't know much about the original inhabitants of Fiji, but Kalou Island boasted one of the oldest civilizations in the world. They lived in unison with the jungle, taking only as much as they needed. They must've known about the snakes. *How could they not?* And again, he wondered if they were feared or worshipped. Perhaps both.

Mark closed his eyes and drifted off to sleep, hoping he would be able to open his eyes again.

A calm, floating sensation overtook Mark. He saw himself as a young child of about seven or eight. He was playing at a house, but it didn't appear like any house he remembered from his childhood. Perhaps somewhere buried so deep inside his mind that it was akin to forgetting it altogether. As he played, he hummed something, though he couldn't tell what the tune was.

Mark's eyes fluttered open. The lights of the city were near. Relief as he'd never felt before washed over him. He lazily rolled his head to the side and watched Riki. Her face was stern, determined. She didn't seem to want any distractions or conversations. She had one goal and focused completely on it. He could see her that way in every facet of her life. A pit bull's determination once she'd decided on something. That must be why she came all the way out here, why she made up elaborate lies and risked her life and reputation exposing lies she deemed greater than her own. Mark decided that despite her lies and manipulations, at her center, she was a good person.

"The hospital's not far," she said. "If I remember right."

They entered the city limits, and Mark felt like he could weep if he allowed himself, but he didn't. It would add nothing and wouldn't even be cathartic. Nothing would be, other than lying somewhere quiet for as long as humanly possible.

"Do you notice something off?" Riki stared out her

driver's side window and the windshield.

Mark surveyed the buildings and cafés as they passed. Everything looked to be in order, until he noticed there were no people. Not a single one.

The windows of one of his favorite restaurants, a Nepalese place with posters of Mt. Everest on the walls, had been shattered. Food still sat on the tables, and a television was playing on the wall, but no one was inside. The streets were empty as well. Though very late at night, there should've been groups of drunken tourists trying to soak up as much of the city as they could before having to leave.

"Stop the truck and turn the engine off."

"Why? The hospital's—"

"Now, Riki." The agitation in his voice surprised even him. "Please."

She did as he asked. She parked on the side of the road and turned the engine off. They sat in silence a moment before she said, "What?"

"Look."

As though invisible shadows dotted everything within the city, the buildings began to shift, as did parts of the surface streets. Riki's mouth opened, about to say something, but she changed her mind. Mark watched one particular portion of the street farther out, beyond some of the streetlights, that appeared to move. It advanced closer to the light, and he caught just a glimpse of the serpent as it slithered across the street and into another building.

Riki swallowed and leaned back in the seat. "How is that even possible?"

"Craig was wrong. We didn't disturb them. They've declared war on us."

Now that they knew what to look for, they saw snakes everywhere. In doorways, crawling down from rooftops, in dark alleys, and wrapped tightly around themselves on the floors of shops. They had taken over the city.

"All those people..." she mumbled.

"There's too many of them to kill all of them. They must've fled."

"Where?"

Mark thought a moment. "The ocean. They probably took as many boats as they could and fled to one of the other islands." He looked at her. "We need to do the same. There's nothing here now."

"How many of them do you think survived?"

"I don't know. We can think about that later. We have to get off this island." He peered out the windows again. "The truck's too loud. We have to move quietly. Or we can gun it down to the docks and see if we can make it."

"I don't know about you, but I don't think I'll be getting out of this truck for anything."

He looked out the passenger side window into a café. It appeared clear, nothing inside. "This place has a backdoor that goes right to the hotel. We can lock ourselves up in a room there on one of the higher floors. Figure out what to do next."

She shook her head. "I think we should just stay here."

"I don't know that much about snakes, but I'm guessing eventually they'll figure out we're here with those damn tongues of theirs. I'd rather be in a hotel with small hallways and only one window in the room."

They were quiet for a long time, watching the city before them writhing in the darkness.

"Okay," she said.

"Come out on my side." Mark, as slowly as possible, pulled the interior door handle. When the door loosened, he pushed it open inch by inch until there was enough room for him to get out. He slid off the seat and touched down lightly with his shoes. He held the door with one hand and with the other beckoned for Riki to follow. She hesitated at first then followed him out.

Once they were both outside, he pointed to their shoes. He slipped his off first, and she did the same. They walked as silently as possible into the café.

The interior was airy and lit well, belying the horror that must've happened here. Old drinks and plates of food littered the tables. Whatever had happened here occurred at least a day ago.

They sneaked around to the kitchen, and it appeared empty. The chrome countertops glistened in the light. *The light.* The electricity—if the snakes had attacked the plant as well, they wouldn't have it for much longer. The last place in the world Mark wanted to be was in the middle of a darkened city with those things.

They hurried past the kitchen, and Mark froze in his tracks. Riki was about to say something, but he held his finger to his lips. Slowly, his gaze drifted to the other side of the kitchen. A thick, black snake curled up tightly near the oven. Not as large as the other ones, perhaps ten or fifteen feet total and the width of a basketball. A baby.

A protrusion that looked like had swallowed a sack of bricks swelled the middle of the body. But through the thin translucent skin, Mark made out a hand and five digits pressing against the flesh of the snake, a motionless posture of the dead. The snake had eaten recently. But as Mark had seen, they would regurgitate their food in order to eat again. He didn't understand why or care right now.

All he cared about was getting past it without that thing moving.

"One step at a time, slowly. Don't run," he whispered.

They headed for the door. The tiled kitchen floor was cool through Mark's socks, and he felt every crack and imperfection, as though the entire world became one large sensory experience of which he couldn't ignore any part. He was acutely aware of the beads of sweat rolling down his back. Of the pain in his hips, back, and legs. The throbbing in his head that hadn't gone away. Even his teeth had started to ache.

And as his gaze locked with the monster in front of him, all of that went away.

The snake's eyes were the size of tennis balls, and they took him in passively. They displayed no emotion at all. Not even apathy. Just two black holes in the snake's head that exhibited nothing. No personality, no soul, just an empty darkness that revealed nothing to the outside world.

Mark and Riki had reached the door when the snake's tongue flicked out for the first time. Immediately afterward, as though it had opened its eyes for the first time, the snake began to uncoil.

"Run!"

They slammed through the doors and into the pantry. Riki inadvertently crashed into a shelf of pots, pans, and dishes, several tumbling to the floor. The noise, forgotten immediately as a minor inconvenience under normal circumstances, was deafening.

The pure horror of it widened her eyes as she realized she would be attracting the attention of others. Mark grabbed her hand and pulled her away. They jumped through the back door. Mark didn't look around, didn't survey what was near him and what was not. He had the hotel in his sights, and he intended to focus only on that.

The façade of the hotel was normal, nothing out of the ordinary. As though it were just another business day. Mark was all the way to the door before he heard the harsh hissing behind them, but he didn't turn around. He opened the door, pushed Riki through, then followed, slamming it shut behind them. He held the door a moment, but nothing happened. He let go, and they raced through the lobby to the elevator. Mark hit the button going up then scanned the hallway. Nothing.

The elevator opened, and they hurried on. They headed up to the eighth floor, as high as they could get. When the elevator doors opened, Mark poked his head out and looked down both sides of the hall. Empty. Several chairs and couches were arranged in front of the elevators. Without planning it, Mark collapsed onto one. Complete exhaustion was eating away at everything, even his thoughts.

"What're we going to do?" Riki asked.

"I don't know. We just need somewhere safe that we can think for a minute."

Riki sat down across from him. No sooner had she done so than they heard a thump from down the hallway. They stared at each other a moment, then Mark grudgingly stood up. He eased past the elevators to where he thought the noise had come from, a set of double doors marked MAINTENANCE and a knob. Mark touched the knob, feeling the smooth metal in his hand, then turned. It clicked open and unlocked. He took a deep breath and opened the door a crack.

At least ten people huddled as tightly as they could in the small space. They must've been in there for some time, with the single lightbulb turned off, because most of them were shielding their eyes, unused to anything but darkness.

Mark recognized one of them. It was the man he had interviewed about Stanley's disappearance. Miguel something.

"You guys all right?" Mark asked.

Miguel rose from the floor. "I remember you."

Mark nodded. "Is there anyone else on this floor?"

"We don't know. Those things attacked, and we jumped in here." He swallowed. "We heard… terrible things. Screaming and crying." He looked at the floor as though embarrassed. "But we couldn't do anything. We just hid in here."

"There was nothing you could've done. Right now, though, we need figure out a way to get off this island. Didn't you say you had a boat?"

"Yeah, but it's at the docks. We'd never make it with those things. You should've seen how fast they took over the city. It was like…"

"I know. If we could make it to your boat, could you fit all of us?"

"Yes."

Mark studied each of the people clustered together for familiar faces but saw none. They were all tourists, not a single local among them. "The entire island's infested with them. We have to get outta here. Eventually, they'll find us here. They use their tongues to find us. We can't hide from them for very long."

Miguel took a step forward, squinting as the light from the hallway fully hit his eyes. "I'll go."

"Anyone else that wants to come can." Mark looked at them again. Only one couple stood up, a man and woman in their forties, and stepped out into the hallway. Everyone else remained where they were.

"If you're going to stay, then stay here and don't leave. I'll send help as soon as we get to the next island. Is everyone certain they're going to stay here?"

No one moved. He stepped out, waiting a moment for anyone to change their mind, then shut the door.

"The docks aren't that far," Mark said. "We have a truck. We could get there in less than five minutes."

"These things can swim," Miguel said.

"We'll have to worry about that later. I know these waters, and I've never seen them. If they do go out into the ocean, they go deep."

Inside a glass case in the hallway were a fire extinguisher and an axe. Mark broke the glass with his elbow, sending shards over the carpet, and pulled out the axe. "There's something I have to do first."

42

The café appeared as quiet and empty as before. Mark left everyone in the pantry. He casually strolled across the pantry, the axe in his hand, pushed open the door to the kitchen, and peered inside.

The snake was curled firmly, its head resting on its body. The tongue was flicking out, and Mark wondered if snakes slept.

He rushed through the door, grunted, and lifted the axe over his head. He swung down with everything he had and caught the snake just behind the head. The blade imbedded itself halfway through. The animal screamed in a way he'd never heard anything other than a person scream.

The snake's body whipped open, wrapping around Mark's legs in a flash. Mark pulled the axe out. He had one more shot at the most. He raised the axe and came down nearly in the same spot as before.

The blade hit the tile of the kitchen floor. He had severed the head from the body, but the body was still twisting and writhing, blood shooting out over the room from the ragged wound. The body slammed into the floor several times, lifting itself back up, and then finally slowed and stopped.

Mark stood still, his heart beating so hard he thought it might break out of his chest. He lay the axe down on a counter and stumbled back to the pantry. "Let's go."

Everyone followed him in silence. They made their way to the dining area then out into the warm air. The truck was untouched. He looked at Riki, who pulled out the keys. Miguel helped the couple into the bed before getting in himself, and Mark took the passenger seat again.

Riki's hand hesitated over the ignition. "Are you sure?"

"No."

She took a deep breath and started the truck. When she pulled away, she did it slowly, keeping the rumble of the engine as low as possible. Once she hit the street, she sped up.

The streets were completely empty. No one anywhere.

"There might be other survivors," Mark said.

"We can't do anything for them right now. We have to call in someone to help them."

Mark didn't argue. In his state, swinging an axe twice had nearly done him in. He couldn't imagine searching a city and trying to dodge those things at the same time.

They reached the docks. No people were around, and more importantly, no snakes. Riki parked the truck as close to the boats as she could. They got out wordlessly and waited for Miguel. "It's that one." He pointed to a yacht moored to a slip.

The nearest island was only about ten miles directly west, with a few major cities. Mark knew how to get there with nothing but a compass. Then they would notify the police about what had happened. Maybe the media, too. The police usually didn't do anything unless the public pressured them. From there, it would be their problem.

Stanley's boat was moored just a few slips down. Mark thought about the poor bastard. Probably snatched right from his boat and eaten there, or maybe dragged into the water like some slimy fish and devoured in the darkness.

Miguel hopped onto his yacht and helped the others aboard. Mark sat on the transom because he didn't want to walk anywhere else. He leaned his head back and watched the night sky lightening with the coming morning. By the time the sun was up, he would be on a different island, in a warm hospital bed.

"Well now, ain't this a sight."

The voice sent a shiver up Mark's back. Before he even consciously put a name and face to it, he knew who it was. Steven stepped onto the yacht. He held a rifle in his hands and rested against the handrails.

"What do you want, Steven? It's over. This whole thing is over."

"It ain't over yet. See, we got us a team on the way. Clean-up team. Keep all this nice and under wraps. Result of an earthquake, maybe. Something like that."

"Earthquake? No one's going to believe this was a natural disaster."

"People will believe what their televisions tell them to believe. And what's more plausible: giant prehistoric snakes ate everyone, or there was an earthquake?"

Anger rushed through him. "That's insane. You can't seriously think you're going to get away with this."

"Money buys whatever you want it buy. Silence is actually pretty cheap." Steven pointed the rifle at him. He looked over at the other people on the vessel then turned his gaze back.

"So you're going to kill me?" Mark said.

"Afraid so, brother. Need you to come with me for now."

"So go ahead and—"

Steven wasn't the type of man to talk. He was the type of man to take action first. If he was talking, action wasn't possible. "You don't have any rounds left," Mark said. "You would've just shot me from the docks if you could've. That's why you're standing here talking."

Steven aimed the rifle at Mark's face. "You ready to bet your life on that?"

The possibility existed that he was wrong. That, as exhausted as he was, he just wasn't thinking right. But it didn't matter. Mark was sick of this. Sick of this island, sick of Steven, sick of everything he had experienced. If he were going to die, at least he would die on his own terms.

He jumped up and rushed at Steven, but no gunshots came. Steven swung with the butt of the rifle and caught him in the jaw, causing him to fall back. Still no gunshots came. Mark had been right. He'd run out of rounds, probably shooting at the snakes.

Steven exhaled loudly. "Good guess, Marky Mark. But it don't mean a thing." He pulled out his hunting knife. "Still gonna have to take you out."

A rush of water sounded near the boat, like a submarine coming to the surface. A foam spray hit the two men as a wave crashed onto the deck. Something was rising. Something huge.

Steven turned just as the head arose.

The head alone was the size of the truck they'd just

driven here in. Mark pictured the body, black and glistening in the light of the rising sun, reaching the bottom of the ocean. It was larger than any animal Mark had ever seen, and it was fixated on them.

Mark rolled to his stomach and leaped away just as the head crashed down into the deck. It swallowed Steven without delivering a single bite, and the head thundered through the fiberglass and wood as though they were children's toys. It lifted itself and withdrew. The yacht lurched as the snake disappeared into the depths again.

"Off the boat!"

Mark helped everyone off as the yacht sank. Only Stanley's boat looked familiar, and Mark ran to it, everyone else following. Another spray of foamy water and the snake was up again, over the sinking yacht. Its tongue, the width of a man, flicked out as it homed in on its prey.

It slammed down again into another boat, the crackle of wood echoing in the air as the ship began to sink. Mark jumped onto Stanley's boat, yelling at the others to head back to the truck. He knew Stanley's way of fishing. The old man preferred to use dynamite to fishing poles. In the early morning hours, before the police department even opened or other tourists were out, Mark heard the bubbling explosions.

He raced below deck as the sea erupted again behind him. Below deck were crates of dynamite, lying out in boxes as if nothing more than old souvenirs or clothing. Mark scoured the bedroom for a lighter or matches and found a lighter in a drawer with a carton of cigarettes.

Before he could reach the dynamite, the boat violently rocked to port, immediately filling with water. It had felt like a plane landed on the ship. It threw Mark against the wall, and he crashed into the floor, already saturated with two feet of water. He pulled himself to his feet and trudged to the crates of dynamite. He took as many sticks as he could carry and strapped them together with duct tape from one of the crates. Holding the bundle high, ensuring the fuses didn't get wet—not that he was sure it mattered—he climbed back up the steps as the boat tilted to starboard and began to be sucked into the ocean.

The snake was at the bow, as though waiting for him. The sight of a creature that large filled him with terror. He hadn't known it was possible for things to grow that big.

The creature didn't look real against the backdrop of the sea. Its eyes, the size of globes, observed its surroundings. The beast was something from the deep past, something primordial that struck a chord of horror. The fangs protruded as its mouth opened and released the most horrifying sound Mark had ever heard. A screech that could make his ears bleed.

He lit the fuses.

As they crackled and burned, he thought of his daughter. That one day, she would think back to her memories of him and smile. That she would raise her own children with the principles he had taught. To be honest, to help others, and always to do what she loved. That last one had been his mistake. He'd gone into a career he didn't love because he thought it would impress his father. The same thing would not happen to her. She was strong. Stronger than he ever was. And a sense of peace that she would be just fine in this world imbued him.

But she still needed her father. And he would be there for her. No damned animal was going to take that away from her.

As the fuses burned, he tossed the lighter over the water, the snake hissing and shrieking at him.

"You want me?" He sprinted toward the snake, his feet pounding against the deck, the sea wind against his face. "Come get me, you son of a bitch!"

The snake opened its jaws and rushed forward, its mouth like a gaping, infected wound, pink and black, rimmed a dark red. The mouth opened, releasing another screech as the snake lifted itself and barreled down on him. Mark tossed the explosives inside just as the enormous black maw nearly enveloped him. He jumped to the side, narrowly missing the head as it crashed through the deck, splintering wood and fiberglass.

Mark leapt over the side of the boat. The snake whipped itself around, its mouth agape as it rushed toward Mark. A black demon that swam through existence. Fearless, without the slightest hint of hesitation. A screech escaped its throat as it arched over the boat, anticipating sinking its fangs into flesh.

Just as it was about to close around him, a deafening boom echoed through air. The explosion was like lightning striking him. Intense heat on his back as though he were being cooked in an oven. The instant singeing of his hair, the frying of his skin. And the impact that threw him forward like a doll.

The ocean was cool against his skin. He struck against it hard and swallowed the briny seawater, choking before it submerged him. The corpse of the snake sizzled, the enormous girth splashing behind him. It slowly sank into the murk, a writhing monster dragged back to where it came from.

Still under water, he looked up. Down here, it was

quiet. Almost peaceful. He just stared at the blue sky, the pain in his back letting him know he was at least still alive, and he closed his eyes as a swell carried him back.

43

Riki Howard was released from the hospital in the capital city of Suva after only a day of observation. They had been worried about shock, but that didn't appear to be an issue. They gave her a sedative to help her sleep and sent her on her way. She threw the sedative into a trash bin and left the hospital.

She called a cab and asked for Nausori Airport. The cabby drove her there in silence, and she preferred it that way. She didn't feel like saying anything to anyone right now.

That morning, she'd read the news reports online. They were calling it the "Disaster of Kalou Island." A massive earthquake had rocked the small island, the article said, killing scores of people and injuring scores of others. VN had sent in hundreds of crews to assist in the clean up and humanitarian aid, the article continued. Doing its part to help those in need.

Humanitarian aid.

The article had made her physically ill. She felt nauseated all morning and consumed some crackers and Sprite to calm her stomach after that. In the end, it didn't matter. They would say whatever they were going to say, and slowly, stories would come out from survivors questioning the veracity of VN's version of events. At first, they would be considered conspiracy theorists, viewed as crazy or with an agenda. But as more and more came out, people would start questioning what happened. And then investigations would open up, and at some point, someone in VN wouldn't be able to take the guilt anymore. The whole thing would come out. The truth always did.

As they passed the beach on the way to the airport, a group of children gathered on the shore staring at something farther out. "Stop here, please," she said. The cabbie pulled over.

The children were fixated on something off the beach, and Riki could see it, too. A whale—a humpback, it looked like—with her calf. The massive tail lifted and splashed down to the delight of the children, their laughter and squeals filling the air.

Riki smiled. "Okay. Let's go."

At the airport, she entered the terminal and saw a figure standing by the metal detectors. Mark, leaning on a cane, smiled at her. They hadn't wanted to release him from the hospital, as he'd suffered some serious burns, but she had a feeling he wasn't about to miss this.

As she approached him, she couldn't help but grin. "Hey," she said.

"Hey."

With that, he took her hand and wordlessly led her outside. The elation was like a fire in her belly, somewhere between excitement and anxiety. She had never been a spontaneous person, and about a million things that could go wrong rushed through her mind. But in the end, none of that mattered. It felt right, and that was good enough for her.

As she walked out of the terminal, she threw her plane ticket back to the States in the trash, never letting go of his hand.

Made in the USA
San Bernardino, CA
06 August 2020